COLOURS OF HOPE AND DESPAIR

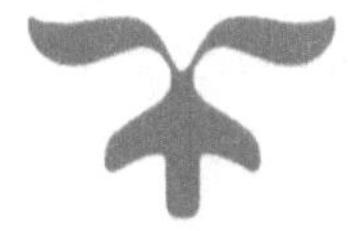

BALA MUDALY

Tale

First published in Australia in 2018 by Tale Publishing

Race to Notting Hill first published in "A View from the Hill" (2017)
Self Inflicted Pain of the Writer's Kind first published in *The Victorian Writer* Aug/Sep 2017

Printed and bound in Australia by Ingramspark.
ISBN: 978-0-6483273-0-1

For all aspiring writers who strive
to bring the perfect story to life.

We have no reason to exist other than to tell stories: funny, serious, true, fabricated. A story is a place where truth and the imagination work together to create emotional and artistic meaning.

Catherine Cole: Seabirds Crying in the Harbour Dark, UWA Publishing 2017.

Writers ought to use language to create awareness about people and problems, to liberate them with the power of words.

Satendra Nandan: Dispatches from Distant Shores, 2017.

Table of Contents

RACE TO NOTTING HILL

Port Phillip District 1853

Drays and carts were to race Mr Cobb's newly acquired Concord Coach, the first of its kind in Port Phillip Colony. The race was to be run from Oakleigh Village to Notting Hill. It had the blessing of Governor La Trobe himself, as he hoped it would lift the spirits of the settlers who'd fallen on hard times. Mr Swanson, a wealthy businessman, had pledged the grand sum of twenty guineas to whomever won the race.

The rule was that only vehicles which reached Oakleigh by nine o'clock that evening could enter the race. Many people took bets on which vehicle would win. Others said it was all too obvious the coach would be a certainty.

A large crowd gathered on the banks of the Yarro-

Yarro on the first Sunday morning in January 1853 and gave the competing vehicles a rousing send off.

Arriving in Oakleigh Village

It was dark as an outdoor dunny at night when Grandpa's coach finally arrived in Oakleigh Village. Nanna, Martha and I hugged and kissed in great relief. What with the dust, sweaty heat and constant jolting on rough gravel, Nanna called the journey a hell run. Grandpa pulled on the reins while Nunga, his native helper and horse whisperer, murmured soothingly to the two horses. The coach slowed and finally stopped. I peered out the window and spotted flickers of lamplight. Voices could be heard. Uncle Lenny, who had ridden all the way on his horse Chomp Chomp, helped us three to get down. Nanna could barely stand, so Martha, her native helper, and I supported her on either side. It was so comforting to be standing again on solid ground. Confined for almost eight hours in the heat and dust of a January day had exhausted us. We were thirsty and desperate for a good feed, a good wash and hours of rest. As my eyes became accustomed to the dark, I noticed a few tents pitched in a small clearing near a line of mounds, each marked with a simple wooden cross. The place gave me the shivers.

'Are we to stay the night in a graveyard?' I whispered to Uncle Lenny, tugging at his coat, hoping those buried there would not hear me.

'This is as safe a place as any, Pippa,' he assured me. 'Not likely to be attacked by natives or kangaroos. The fire will burn through the night and we'll be in the company of friendly folk.'

Looking out towards where Uncle Lenny was pointing, I noticed men seated near the tents smoking and drinking, a small pit fire lighting up their bearded faces.

Three large women holding candles hurried to us. 'Welcome ladies. You must be with Mr Cobb?' The first lady introduced herself as Mrs Atkinson.

'Don't worry as we'll take good care of you all,' she lisped, her mouth bereft of teeth. Nanna thanked the women profusely.

After we had taken turns in the dunny, each of us savoured a good wash and, thereafter, bowls of steaming chicken broth, which brought on the yawns. I was barely awake when I crawled into a tent pitched near the line of graves. Nanna lay on a swag next to me. Uncle Lenny and Grandpa had the next tent, while Martha and Nunga preferred to sleep in the open close to the pit fire under the star-filled sky.

~

The insistent laughter of a kookaburra woke me. Nanna, however, was still tossing and turning in troubled sleep.

'Are you and Nanna awake, Pippa?' It was Uncle

Lenny calling from outside our tent. 'The race starts soon.'

I hurried to tidy myself. Mrs Atkinson's helper brought me a dish of water and a cloth. All the while I worried about Nanna. As if she had read my mind, Mrs Atkinson stuck her head into the tent to check on us.

'Your Nanna's still asleep? I can tell she's an ill woman in need of much rest and healing. This is where she'll remain until tomorrow when I expect you'll return from Notting Hill, when this foolish race is done.' I felt so relieved Nanna was in good hands.

Having instructed Martha to stay back and care for Nanna, Grandpa turned to me. The moment's silence seemed to last forever. I wrung my hands hunting for the right words with which to plead my case to go on the coach all the way to Notting Hill.

'Pippa dear, it isn't proper for you to travel without female company,' said Grandpa.

'Surely Pippa is our responsibility, Mr Cobb,' intervened Uncle Lenny. 'We can't burden Mrs Atkinson unduly.' Grandpa chewed on the end of his unlit cigar.

'Please Grandpa, I'll be no problem. Please! I so want to see you win the race. And I'll be the only woman there to tell people, from real experience, how comfortable coach travel is.'

That decided it for Grandpa. He smiled, clearly

persuaded by the vision of his Concord Coach arriving in Notting Hill to wild cheers and merriment with the competing drays nowhere to be seen. Uncle Lenny helped me into the coach and then handed me a basket with damper, pieces of carrot, and a flagon of cider. 'Compliments of Mrs Atkinson,' he said winking.

All Set To Go

The competitors assembled before Mr Atkinson who was to adjudicate the race. From the vantage point of the coach window, I had the best view of everything. There were four men in all, including Grandpa. He looked tall and distinguished in a top hat, black tailcoat and riding breeches.

'That's Mr Campbell next to Grandpa,' explained Uncle Lenny who stood at the coach window holding Chomp Chomp by the reins while puffing on his pipe. 'Operates a transport business, he does. The race was actually his idea. He's out to discredit Grandpa, who believes coaches will soon be the most popular transport in Port Phillip District'

'I hope he doesn't win the race,' I blurted.

'Then there is Mr Rodney, the baker,' continued Uncle Lenny. 'And next to him is the man who calls himself Jefferson.'

'Oh! So he's Mr Jefferson is it? That mad man shot past Grandpa yesterday on the Damper Track from Melbourne. He almost caused an accident.' It made me angry simply remembering the incident. The man still had no hat to protect him from the fierce sun, having lost it when it fell into the creek while he was overtaking our Concord. He looked weary now and out of place, as if he hadn't slept or eaten for many days. I wondered who he really was and why he had entered the race. 'Could he be an escaped convict?' I asked.

'Hush, not so loud, Pippa. True, the man's a stranger to us. Newly arrived in Melbourne, he says. But let not our fear and anger lead us to hasty conclusions.'

'Now gentlemen, hear me out,' said Mr Atkinson, the husband of our caring host. An eager and excited crowd of adults and children had gathered in front of the line of graves. Nanna and Martha stood near Mrs Atkinson, their faces showing how worried they were for my safety.

'You'll likely find the track to Notting Hill more challenging and treacherous than the run from Melbourne, what with stray animals, boulders and an occasional fallen tree,' Mr Atkinson continued. 'Look to your own safety and respect your fellow competitors.' Mr Atkinson would certainly be knowledgeable of the local terrain since he was in charge of the pound for stray animals at Scotchman's Creek.

Grandpa and the others nodded.

'In conclusion,' said Mr Atkinson, 'may I add that anyone who cheats or intentionally endangers others will be disqualified from the race and reported to the colony's constabulary. I hope I make myself abundantly clear.' He looked fixedly in the direction of Mr Jefferson who, at that moment, seemed engrossed in his battered boots. 'I'll now ride ahead and await your arrival in Notting Hill at Wilkinson's Grocery Store & Bakery. My good wife will start you off.' With that, Mr Atkinson mounted his horse and rode away. Uncle Lenny mounted Chomp Chomp in readiness to ride ahead of Grandpa and be his scout.

The Race

Mrs Atkinson raised the Union Jack in her right hand and waited until the competitors were seated in their vehicles with taut reins in hand. At the fall of the flag, the two drays, the baker's cart and the Concord Coach burst into motion, prompting cheers, cat-calls and clouds of dust, which billowed over the spectators. They scattered, coughing and spluttering. Thankfully, I was spared. The baker's cart, being the lightest, bolted ahead. Grandpa kept up a furious pace, with the two drays close behind.

'You going well, Mr Cobb,' I heard Nunga say. 'Them drays lost far behind.'

'Yeah. Luck be with us, we'll be in Notting Hill before noon sipping beer. You mark my word.'

Uncle Lenny, who was riding ahead of the coach, returned to advise Grandpa that the track in front was dangerously narrow in parts with unexpected sharp bends. 'I'll ride behind you for a bit as not to hinder your progress,' he said. Nunga urged his horses with soothing sounds. We made steady progress. The coach rushed on and on, over ruts and bumps and patches of loose gravel, dodging tree stumps and large rocks. The heat and dust made breathing quite difficult. I held on as best I could, and sang under my breath to keep me calm.

Suddenly the world collapsed around us like we were hit by an earthquake. In a frightening second, the coach lurched sideways and came to a violent stop throwing me onto the floor. Nunga screamed in alarm and Grandpa shouted, 'Oh bugger me, Oh bugger me!'

Dizzy, I struggled to lift myself up but couldn't do so as the vehicle was tilted to one side. My left elbow bled from a slight grazing. The next minute Uncle Lenny reached into the coach, eased me out and rested me gently on the dirt. I was dazed and unsure what had happened.

'There's been a little accident, Pippa. Nothing too serious for you to fret over. Grandpa and I are sorting it out. Close your eyes now and rest a little.'

I was just about dozing off when voices close by alerted me, and I sat up. Grandpa and Uncle Lenny were talking in low voices. They looked troubled.

Grandpa's top hat was crumpled and there was dirt on his jacket. Nunga was close by in the shade of a tea tree carefully inspecting the two horses, which he had unhitched. His face and hands were covered in dirt and his shirt was shredded at the side. I limped close to them. Grandpa put his arm around my shoulders and drew me close. 'I'm so relieved you're not seriously hurt, dear. I only wish I hadn't brought you along.'

A warm wind disturbed the tall gums making them creak and complain.

We all stood in shock taking in our misfortune. The coach had spun off the track and lay to one side. What shocked us was seeing the baker's cart nearby as well, badly damaged and blocking the track. It was still hitched to the horse, which was crumpled and lifeless. An emaciated dead cow lay partly under the cart. Waves of frantic flies covered both dead animals. I became tearful and looked away.

'It's obvious what happened,' observed Uncle Lenny, 'The baker's cart ploughed into that wretched cow, a likely stray from Mr Atkinson's Pound. Mr Rodney then shot his wounded horse and took off.'

'I rounded this here blind bend at a great pace,' explained Grandpa, 'and crashed into the abandoned cart. It was like colliding into a mountain face in fog. That infernal baker deserves to hang. Surely he could have warned us before fleeing.'

'In truth, I'm the guilty one, Mr Cobb,' moaned Uncle Lenny. 'As your eyes and ears, I should have stayed ahead of the coach and alerted you.'

The two drays caught up with us. Mr Campbell was appalled to see the coach stranded in the middle of the track in a calamitous state, so much so that he stopped his dray, dismounted and hastened over to enquire what had happened. Mr Jefferson, on the other hand, hesitated a moment, slowing his dray just enough to scan us over, with eyes as dreary as an overcast winter's morning. Then he drove on in silence, carefully avoiding the coach, the baker's cart and the dead animals.

'You'll still stay in the race Mr Cobb, won't you?' asked Mr Campbell, shaking his head in disbelief.

'Not possible,' answered Grandpa casting a despondent gaze at his precious Concord, listing with a buckled front wheel. He sounded defeated and humbled. I felt sorry for him.

'Any assistance I can give you, before moving on?'

'Not really, Mr Campbell. But we'd appreciate some tonic. And thanks for your concern. To interrupt your run merely to help us is a most gallant act.'

'We'll secure the coach and follow you on our

horses,' added Uncle Lenny.

'Don't let that Jefferson fellow get the better of you,' was Grandpa's advice to the departing Mr Campbell.

A Surprise

I sat behind Uncle Lenny on Chomp Chomp with my legs dangling to one side, while holding onto Uncle Lenny's waist. Grandpa and Nunga rode on the two horses unhitched from the coach. We proceeded slowly, careful not to get into more difficulties. The track rose steadily towards the hills causing the horses to strain and sweat in the heat.

Wilkinson's Grocery Store and Bakery was located on a hillside next to a clump of mountain ash. Even from a distance we could tell that a dozen or so people had gathered there. Some stood on the timber veranda of the store and others on the steps to the entrance. It was early afternoon, and the heat was at its peak. One of the drays made towards us, raising a trail of dust. A couple of yelping mongrel dogs followed, attempting to outrun the dray. It was Mr Atkinson and Mr Campbell come to commiserate.

'If it weren't for the accident, the Concord would certainly have outrun the drays and cart,' said Mr Campbell as he turned his dray around. 'But then,' he added as an afterthought, 'fortune is such a fickle thing. Wouldn't you say?

Reaching the store, we were taken aback to see Mr Rodney. He limped to Grandpa as soon as we dismounted and apologised profusely. 'Didn't mean to cause you grief, Mr Cobb. You must believe me. How will I ever make amends?' He wrung his hands and wiped his brow, both arms and face covered in angry blisters.

'Come now, Mr Rodney, you weren't at fault. Not at all. What happened to us was an act of God. Let's leave it at that.' And I'd thought Grandpa intended to box his ears!

'Thanks, Mr Cobb, you're a considerate man like that there Mr Jefferson who found me lying on the exposed track in a parlous state and stopped and collected me.' Grandpa and Uncle Lenny raised their eyebrows and exchanged looks of surprise and disbelief.

Mr Atkinson mounted the stairs, took up a vantage point on the veranda and cleared his throat. All this while, Mr Jefferson was seated on a step, his knees pulled up to his chin and his head resting on his folded arms. One of the mongrels was now stretched out asleep on the lower step, ears twitching. 'Ladies and gentlemen, it falls upon my shoulders today to announce the winner of the race, a truly astounding result.

'I wish he would be brief and have it done with,' mumbled Grandpa.

'Come up here Mr Jefferson,' invited Mr

Atkinson. The man obliged with little visible enthusiasm. 'Ladies and gentlemen, Mr Jefferson's dray was first to arrive at Wilkinson's Grocery Store and Bakery.' With that he hoisted Mr Jefferson's reluctant right hand into the air. A few in the crowd clapped in an uncertain manner. Mr Jefferson burst into sobs, his shoulders heaving in spasms. I didn't feel sympathetically disposed.

'If I may take the liberty of explaining Mr Jefferson's emotional state,' continued Mr Atkinson. 'The poor man has been burdened by enormous pain and suffering since the loss of his wife to consumption. Now his infant child, bereft of a mother, is ill with croup.'

Muffled sympathetic comments were heard. 'Mr Jefferson's been driven by desperation to find money to pay for medical treatment for his child, for baby feed and to hire a wet nurse.' Mr Atkinson paused, wiped his brow and gazed past us as if he had stumbled upon a profound truth.

Mr Jefferson at his side stopped sobbing and raised his head for the first time, presenting us a forlorn face. A flood of shame washed over me.

'So you see now,' concluded Mr Atkinson 'how the Almighty works His will in mysterious ways. Mr Jefferson here was clearly destined to win the twenty guineas pledged by Mr Swanson.'

'Amen' rose in unison from the crowd and, almost spontaneously, we all began singing

‘Amazing Grace’, our voices rising up from Notting Hill and lifting into the surrounding forest of eucalyptus and mountain ash. Noisy kookaburras fell silent, and a family of grazing kangaroos raised their heads and, momentarily, stood alert. Grandpa’s voice, now clearly distinct, floated above all ours and echoed in the hills beyond.

I never felt so good.

~

HIPPOPOTAMI

'What's new your way?' asked the ancient
man
Dark against the mid-day sun.
'Hippopotami,' I replied,
Pointing the way I'd come.
Hippopotami?
Incredulity creased his bearded face
As he passed me by
On his tall camel
Chewing and nodding,
Giving me the evil eye.
The lurid sun whirled and swirled,
Felled me off my high seat
Into the sea of shifting sand.
My camel bolted in fright.

His, turned and snorted
In disgust.

DARK IS THE COLOUR OF NIGHT

Isaac sat up in bed and scratched his head to get oriented. The 6am news came on automatically. 'It's a chilly Friday morning,' announced the woman in a cheerful radio voice. Doesn't worry me, he thought, except when the wretched arthritis attacks. But Katia simply dreaded winter. I better get the fire going by noon, he reminded himself, so it's warm enough when I bring her home.

The phone rang and rang, but Isaac was oblivious to it. A single hearing aid sat on a shelf nearby. He was now fully absorbed in making almond biscuits. This was his daily morning routine since his daughters had their mother admitted to an aged-care nursing home two years ago.

'Dad be realistic', they had insisted, 'at your age

you're no longer able to care for her full-time. But there's no reason why Mum can't come visiting almost daily.'

She's definitely going downhill, he had to admit. Falling off her bed that many times, bound to hurt herself. And her memory gone. Her best friend Agnes died the other day and she had no clue who I was talking about. Her turn will come soon enough, I guess. Isaac slumped into a chair and stared at the floor for a whole minute before he picked himself up with resolve and returned to his almond biscuits.

The aroma of baking lifted Isaac's spirits. It also displaced the mustiness of a poorly aired house. He stepped out and gathered a few logs from the woodheap near the back door, depositing them in a basket at the grate in his lounge. Next, he knelt and cleaned the fire-place, collecting the previous night's ash in a metal bucket, which he also kept nearby. Once he'd got the fire going, he shaved, showered, and dressed. He was ready to set off for Hopewell Nursing Home. He reached for his hat, which hung on a hook behind the front door.

Isaac arrived at the nursing home punctually at eleven, just when the daily music therapy was winding up. He scanned the lost and confused faces of elderly residents, many in wheelchairs positioned in a large circle. Katia was not among them. Could she be in the ladies? Just then a young nurse with braided hair and a dark complexion spotted him and came over looking stern.

'Mr Bugalski, we've tried to phone you a few times this morning and you did not answer.'

'Why, is there a problem?' He felt like he was being scolded by one of his daughters.

'Come into the duty office and I'll explain.'

He shuffled behind her down the passage, trying not to lose her in the melee of wheel-chairs spilling out from the lounge. He felt almost out of breath. What's happening to me, he thought, feeling a little foolish. In reality, the passage wasn't that long and the office was easily visible behind a large glass panel from around the corner.

'Take a seat, Mr Bugalski', said the nurse. 'The overnight duty worker phoned you this morning, hoping to speak with you before she left.' The nurse scanned the computer screen as she spoke. 'In any case, her notes here say Katia had a very restless night. A nightmare perhaps. Some fearful thing from her past may have got to her.' She took her eyes off the screen and gave Isaac a reassuring look. 'You know how it is with dementia. The people here are fearful of so many things. Harmless to most of us.'

'So where is Katia now?' said Isaac, indifferent to her opinion. 'I didn't see her in the music room.'

'Deep asleep, I guess. At least she was half an hour ago. That's when I last checked on her.'

'And breakfast?'

'No, she wasn't there.'

She must be starving, worried Isaac. I'll take her to the Oakleigh RSL for a good feed, which will sort her out.

'The night duty nurse phoned to advise you not to come in today. Katia needs time to make up for lost sleep, you know.'

'But can I see her for myself?' he asked looking down at his hat.

'For sure. But don't wake her.' She led the way.

Katia was not in her bed. The nurse gasped.

'You said Katia was asleep?' Isaac said.

As they left the room to find her, a toothless woman in bedroom slippers intercepted them. 'Katia, Katia,' she mouthed, taking Isaac's hand and proceeded towards the dining hall. There, Katia was in her nightwear, hair dishevelled, staring at a large wall calendar while babbling in agitation.

'Why aren't you in bed, Katia?' asked the nurse.

Isaac hugged his wife, hoping to get her attention. She looked at him momentarily before fixing her vacant eyes on the calendar again.

'What's it, dear? What is it?' Isaac asked with gentle concern as he followed her attention. It was only then that it struck him it was 13 July. The date on which Katia's mother had drowned herself back in Europe when Katia was only five years old.

'You can see your wife is having one of her bad days, Mr Bugalski,' intervened the nurse. 'I suggest you return in the afternoon. We'll put her to bed after a shower and a late breakfast.'

'But I intended to take her out for lunch,' protested Isaac.

'We can't risk that. Not in her present condition.'

Isaac was left standing while Katia was led away. He twisted the brim of his hat as if he knew no other way to wring out his frustration. This was exactly what he feared would happen when his daughters single-mindedly removed her from his loving care. They simply wouldn't listen. They didn't understand.

~

Isaac sat in his lounge thumbing through *The Herald Sun.* He had stoked the fire with two more logs. Reading about the political shenanigans in the country was enough to distract him for a while from his aches and pains, his loneliness and the relentless worry over his wife. At two o'clock, he set off back to the nursing home. He frowned, uncertain what to expect.

He was taken aback but delighted to find Katia loitering in the hallway as if she anticipated him coming to take her out. Her hair was in place. It pleased him to see her rested and freshly dressed in a floral top, cardigan and a warm pair of slacks.

'Hello dear, how nice to see you looking well,' he said hugging her. Katia gave him a puzzled and vacant look, turned and shuffled away. Isaac followed. She was compliant when he took her hand and walked her to the duty station.

'Oh yeah, she seems much better now,' said the day nurse, someone Isaac had not seen before. 'Yes, it's quite okay to take Katia out for the afternoon.'

'She'll like the sun, although it's not that warm out there,' said Isaac. 'I've brought a blanket and a flask of tea.'

'Good on you,' said the nurse as she returned to her paperwork. 'Don't forget, dinner is at six.'

Isaac parked opposite the Oakleigh RSL. A few mothers had ventured out with their toddlers and kinder kids to the playground in Warrawee Park, taking in the little sunshine the day offered. The children ran around with squeals of delight, followed closely by their mothers. Some scrambled to the top of the slide and slid down at daring speeds, landing on their bottoms on a bed of woodchips. Isaac and Katia sat on a bench nearby. The children's liveliness seemed to hold Katia's attention and draw her out of her mental fog. At times Isaac thought he noted a flicker of a smile. He kept talking to her, drawing her attention to life unfolding all around them.

He poured out two enamel mugs of tea from his flask and set them by his side on the bench, then opened his tin of freshly baked almond biscuits and offered it to Katia who looked into the tin but seemed not to know what to do.

'Here Katia,' said Isaac handing her one, 'have one of my biscuits. You'll like these.'

She nibbled at it tentatively. Her eyes drifted aimlessly, no longer drawn to the children. Then all at once she froze, her body stiffened. Her face assumed a grave expression. Isaac sensed the change.

'What is it, dear? You're not liking the cold?' He followed her gaze beyond the boundary of the playground. Only then did he realise a cluster of ancient gravestones, a familiar feature of Warrawee Park, had distracted her. Now he too felt a little unsettled. 'Let's go, dear. I'll take you home. But finish your biscuit.'

As Isaac stepped a few paces to the bin, an emboldened crow hopping nearby, seized the opportunity to snatch the half-eaten biscuit from Katia's hand. She shrieked. The children froze in the midst of play. A man, pushing a pram through the park came over and asked if he could help.

That's about done it, thought Isaac. Better get her to our place this minute. He calmed his wife with soothing words while ensuring full eye contact. 'Come love, let's go home and you can rest in your favourite chair. And there's orange cake for you. Yes, orange cake.' He struggled to get Katia into the car.

As Isaac approached his house, he spotted Kay,

a sickly neighbour from further down the street, seated on his knee-high front wall. She stood up immediately and looked embarrassed for resting there. Isaac stopped as he turned into his driveway and wound down his window.

'Hello Kay. It's a bit cold to be out on a walk. How're you doing?'

'Good, good,' mumbled Kay, raising her head a little and resting her wintery-blue eyes on him. A feeble smile followed. 'So sorry to be sitting on your wall. It's my knees, you know.'

Isaac laughed and assured her it was no problem, as he got out to check for post. Kay was about to push her shopping cart ahead of her when she hesitated for a moment, turned to Isaac.

'Your cat looked a little frantic just then. I saw the poor thing tugging at the curtains, wanting out.'

'A cat? We don't have a cat. You sure it was a cat you saw?'

But Kay had already moved on having reported her concern. Isaac wanted to hurry to check it out just in case Kay *had* seen something but with Katia on his arm, he couldn't.

'Bugger this,' he said, fumbling for the right key. He seldom managed to open the door on the first attempt. He led Katia by the hand into the kitchen. As she lowered herself onto a chair, a huge cat bolted past her from the lounge, knocking over the pedal bin as it sped across the kitchen floor and out through a partially open window. Isaac was almost run over by this apparition in full flight. Katia cried out in fear. Isaac stood transfixed.

Katia began rocking. 'Black cat, black cat,' she wailed.

Isaac was amazed that she could name what she had seen, but alarmed at the same time that the incident might severely unsettle her. Katia had grown up in a family steeped in superstition.

Katia continued to whimper while he hastily made a strong cup of tea for her. But the drink made no difference. Isaac now had misgivings. He shouldn't have brought her home. He helped her into the lounge and settled her on the couch near the fire-place, covering her with a blanket. Only then did he phone the nursing home and report what had happened. 'Is it okay if I bring her back right away?'

'It was a mistake, whoever let you take her out,' was the stern response. 'Don't bother, I'll send someone now to collect her.'

It's the worst day ever, Isaac thought. He poured himself a little brandy to steady his nerves and puzzled over the cat. None of his neighbours had a cat, that much he was certain of. It didn't make sense. Perhaps there were mysteries beyond his understanding.

Isaac telephoned his daughters. Not wanting to alarm them, he merely said their mother was a little unsettled as she appeared to be aware, even in her mental state, it was the anniversary of their grandmother's suicide. For several hours thereafter he kept busy pottering about, attending to little things. He washed several pairs of his underpants, emptied the kitchen bin and wheeled the recycle bin into the street. He cleaned the kitchen sink and sorted his tablets into the seven-day pillbox. That done, he settled down to watch *Lateline* on ABC TV. He rarely turned in before midnight, but tonight was different. He yawned although it was not yet ten. Somewhat reluctantly, he turned off the TV and climbed into bed. The embers in the fireplace had gone out a while ago. He felt comforted snuggled in his blankets. Night asserted itself, dense and pervasive, conspiring with the silent chill of the house.

~

Isaac sat up in alarm. Had he heard Katia falling off the bed? Disoriented, he fumbled for the bedside lamp. It took him a moment to focus. Ah yes, his mind was playing tricks again. She's never coming back, he thought. He flipped off the covers, found his slippers and headed for the bathroom. When he slid back under the blankets and turned to switch off the lamp, he glanced cursorily at the alarm clock. It was just past eleven.

Isaac was up early the next morning and got down to his usual morning routine. I'll make a few muffins for afternoon tea, he thought while vacuuming the kitchen. If Katia is up to it, we'll have lunch at the RSL.

He did not hear the phone ring.

Isaac was in the shower when there was an urgent tapping on the window and a man's voice calling to him. He turned off the shower and grabbed his towel. 'Just a minute. Who's there?'

'Mr Bugalski, I've come with a message for you from Hopewell. I've been knocking on both your front and back doors for the last five minutes.' The man sounded annoyed.

'What is it?'

'It's about your wife.'

'Katia?'

'Yeah. They're upset you didn't answer your phone this morning. They want you at the nursing home this minute.'

Isaac hastened to get there, his hair still damp and dishevelled. What's more, he had forgotten his hat. He was immediately ushered into the duty office, sat down and given a cup of black tea. He felt an ominous tightness in his gut and a scream forming deep within him.

'Katia died in her sleep,' said the nurse in charge as if reporting an everyday event. 'It was about seven when someone went to get her up for breakfast.' Isaac fiddled with his hearing aid. 'We phoned you immediately, you know, Mr Bugalski!'

He looked up. 'Here's a copy of the visiting doctor's report. He puts the time of her death about eleven pm last night – Friday 13th.'

Can't understand why the heating has to be that high, thought Isaac as he stood up to remove his coat. The smell of bacon and burnt toast saturated the air. He wished he was in his vegetable patch just then poking about for slugs.

'Mr Bugalski, have you heard me?'

'So I can't take her out to lunch?' he said almost to himself.

The nurse frowned.

~

A KIND OF BLINDNESS

You there,
See
This here burnt fractured land
Is *Country*
Ancient beyond time.
See how
Ghost gums stand darkly still
Against a star-sprinkled sky,
Ochre-red gorges
In deep, deep mourning.
Creeks and river-beds dry
Show scars of past deluge.
Where burnished spinifex clumps
Keep watch
Over us Mob,

Invisible to you,
At the waterhole.
You careless trekker
Stomping regardless
Turning every mulga tree
Into a lavatory;
Seeing nothing
Knowing nothing.

SHADOW OF PAINFUL THINGS

'A story has no beginning or end.'
It's weird how things pop up in my head at the oddest time. Must have read that somewhere ages ago. Yeah, that's it.

Fiona was at her kitchen table flipping through the pages of the *Gippsland Community Chronicle*, waiting for the kettle to boil. She hesitated when she came upon the Missing Persons column, which this week had photos of two young local women. Accompanying the photos were pleas for information to help the police find them. Their families claimed the women were living normal lives and they had no inkling why they'd disappeared.

None of the Missing Person stories Fiona had closely studied in the *Chronicle* over the years made her any the wiser why her Angus had disappeared in the midst of a loving marriage. She had had months of counselling for grief and depression. 'Remember,' the counsellor had said in the concluding session 'when a loved one vanishes without a trace, pain can linger a lifetime.' How true. Her pain of loss hadn't diminished. Not in all these years. Hers then *was* a never-ending story.

The kettle hissed. Fiona set aside the paper and stepped onto the veranda with her mug of coffee. Bare feet on bare boards. The house became deathly quiet when her present husband, Michael, took off to the milking shed in the early hours and the school bus collected her two children. She dreaded being left on her own.

Out on the veranda, she felt less lonely. The mooing of the milking herd was comforting. So, too, were the magpies flaunting their skills in song. She scanned the paddock now splattered yellow with dandelions. The hills beyond were just visible in the morning haze. She felt settled at Budgaree, their modest dairy farm. Yet would she ever let go of Moe and her past life, she wondered. For the moment, she was absorbed in soothing her arthritic fingers with the warmth of her mug, which she held close to her face, the aroma dancing off its creamy surface. Her life moved in struts, from one day to another. Painful memories assailed her like persistent flies.

It was going on twenty years since Angus vanished from her life. 'Catch you later, love,' he had said one afternoon as he set off for his late shift at the sawmill. His boyish smile always delighted her. They had enjoyed a lazy morning lying in, and had drifted to the local pub for lunch. Lamb shanks and beer. Those last hours were now indelibly etched in her memory – even the fact that she had dropped her fork and splattered gravy on her beige skirt.

The police were of little help and gave up looking after a few weeks, saying he may have simply *taken off*. Consult a psychic, a friend suggested, which she did. She was prepared to try any desperate measure. She even had her family and friends do a poster blitz in the neighbourhood.

Angus would be forty-five now. Forty-five! He may be dead for all I know.

Fiona sighed and returned into the house and got on with her dreary domestic chores as she had done almost every day since meeting Michael and starting a family.

~

One day in October, her husband came home grim-faced from Moe with the monthly shopping. 'The bottom's fallen out of the milk market, hon,' he said, plonking into a chair.

Fiona frowned. 'I don't understand.'

'The large supermarkets are adopting mean

tactics. Many dairy farmers are going to the wall, love. We may have to downsize. I mean, sell a few of the milking herd. And I might have to find a paid job.' A possibility he did not relish.

'Who'll do the milking then? I certainly can't,' she said, raising her voice.

'We'll have to find a farmhand, I guess.' Michael went silent as he unpacked the shopping.

Fiona, picking up on his worry, felt the anxiety rise in her.

Once he'd decided on what precautions to take to secure his family, Michael set about scanning job adverts in local papers. He also let it be known at the local garage and newsagent that he was on the hunt for a farmhand. The garage attendant suggested he put up a "Wanted" ad on their notice board.

'I'm not very hopeful of quick results,' he said to Fiona. 'Some belt-tightening may be necessary. Sorry for the kids.'

Weeks went by with little change. On a rainy Saturday, Michael deposited his children, Matt and Zoe, at the Moe public library while he topped up his ute at the garage. As he crossed the road to the newsagent, the garage attendant called out.

'There's a bloke, a drifter from somewhere, read your farmhand poster. Seemed interested.'

'Is he with you?' said Michael.

'No. I pointed him to May's Kitchen for a cheap

bite. Might still be there. Lean guy in a faded red shirt. Week's stubble. Not likely to miss him'

Fiona was at the sink washing muck off eggs she'd collected from the chook house when her son came bursting in ahead of his dad and little sister to announce they'd found a farmhand.

'Yeah. He's out there in the yard,' he said gesturing with his head. 'Followed us home in a scrappy car.'

Discontinuing what she was doing, Fiona turned and confronted Michael. 'You can't have hired a total stranger, just like that, surely?'

'Sorry, hon, but he seemed so keen. Decent-looking bloke. And experienced he says. Thought I'd show him the ropes before going job-hunting myself.'

'What if he's a fugitive from the police?

She glimpsed the man through the kitchen window. He was strolling in the yard, looking out towards the paddocks, his right hand thrust deep in the side pocket of his washed-out khaki pants and the other, nearer his chest with a cigarette. In between puffs, he let out a deep and chesty cough. The late morning sun picked up his gaunt unshaven profile.

There's something vaguely familiar about the man, thought Fiona. Was it how he moved and held his head? But she dismissed the notion, remembering the number of times in the past she had mistook someone for Angus – once with embarrassing consequence.

'His name's Gus, mum,' said Zoe pleased to add a significant bit to the news.

Angus and *Gus*. How bizarre, though Fiona.

Michael accepted his farmhand as a godsend. For the first few days he stood by observing Gus as he milked the herd. He noted how well the man followed instructions, how he was up early and at his task before Michael arrived to check on him. Gus didn't even look up to greet his boss.

~

Fiona began to relax a little, and once even agreed to accompany Michael and the children to the cinema in Moe. Mindful of his wife's anxious nature, Michael advised his farmhand to keep away from the house. Fiona, therefore, put his lunch tray on a wooden bench in the back veranda. Otherwise, the man fended for himself. She had no idea what he had for breakfast or dinner. Michael made sure that the lean-to for the farmhand was adequately fitted out with a kettle, a gas cooker and utensils.

On occasions, Fiona would spot Gus from her kitchen window walking up from the milking shed to collect his lunch, and at other times his receding back as he returned to his lean-to.

Complications arose from something quite trivial and unforeseen. Little Zoe, from sheer innocence and curiosity, soon developed a habit of visiting Gus whenever she was at a loose end and whenever her dad was away on casual work and her mum and brother were doing their own thing. The farmhand did not discourage her. She'd be standing there barefoot with her impish freckled face squinting in the sunlight and looking all serious. She'd watch him closely as he worked, asking questions, offering suggestions or simply inspecting the man in silence. Fiona or Matt would go and get her. Fiona was never comfortable in discharging this responsibility. Fortunately, Zoe accompanied her mother back to the house with very little fuss. Fiona urged her daughter in a kind but firm manner that she not go down to the shed as it disturbed Gus at his work.

'But mum, I don't worry him,' Zoe would protest. 'I just love to see him do things like milking. He tells me all about his work, how to fix things and about the cows, too. He's given each one names, Mum. I wish girls could do work like Gus.'

'Really, love? But Daddy may not be pleased if Gus fell behind with his work. You know he has a lot to do.' Fiona hugged and kissed her daughter and let the matter rest.

However, when she expressed her concern to Michael, he couldn't see a problem. 'She may learn something useful,' he said. 'In any case, who knows, she may be a successful farmer herself one day.'

Fiona was not entirely persuaded by her

husband's reasoning.

'He coughs and spits all the time. And those cigarette butts are strewn all over. A real risk to Zoe.'

'Come on, hon, give the man a break. It's clear you don't like him.'

The rancid smell of cigarette reminded her of Angus and late-night parties when they were dating. She had so hated his lifestyle but went along all the same. It frightened her to see his mates wrecking their lives. So she'd rescued Angus by marrying him, she reflected. But had she, really?

Now here was this farmhand, his sallow, weathered and unshaven face spoke of neglect, of someone who had lost his way in the world. Fiona flinched. She felt an anger deep within her. For years she had resisted the lurking suspicion that the police might have been right. Angus *had* taken off. Her abiding love hadn't been sufficient to hold him. Michael was correct. She did resent the farmhand's intrusion into her life as it only served to dredge up unwanted memories.

'Have you even considered he may be contaminating the milk?'

Michael, seeing Fiona in one of her unreasonable moods, said nothing.

Late one afternoon a week later when Michael was out and about, Gus turned up at the cottage unannounced. Holding his tray in both hands, lunch untouched, he used his foot to ease the partially opened screen-door. The creaking startled Fiona, who swung around in her kitchen chair. She gave a muffled cry and stared at the intruder.

'Oh, it's you,' she exclaimed between gasps. The tension on her face eased just a fraction in recognition of the intruder, but uncertain of the threat he may pose. The toilet, separated by a wall from the kitchen, dripped noisily and persistently. I must tell Michael to sort it out, she thought. The man before her stood large, taking up almost all the oxygen in the small kitchen. She felt oddly dizzy. An overpowering smell of cows filled the air. Before she could recover her composure and demand an explanation, Gus stepped up.

'Thanks for taking care of me meals, ma'am,' he muttered between coughs, jaws working hard, his troubled eyes now fixed on the tray. 'Couldn't polish off your cooking today. Bit crook, you see.' With that he turned and scuttled off.

Her head was still in a muddle hours later when Zoe and Matt burst into the kitchen, dropped their laden backpacks and scrambled to the fridge for a drink.

'You okay, Mum? Dad's coming,' said Matt making for his room without pausing. Zoe came over and cuddled Fiona.

'I'm sure it was Gus's car I spotted outside Dr Ali's clinic this morning,' said Michael as soon as he entered the kitchen. I told him to have that cough sorted out if he wished to keep his job.'

'Yeah, said he was crook,' said Fiona without elaborating.

'You mean you actually spoke to him this afternoon?'

'Returned his lunch untouched.'

'That's odd. I don't see his car. Gus must have got back from the doctor's and taken off again.'

Fiona frowned.

The evening slid into bedtime, still there was no sign of the farmhand. Fiona peeked out the kitchen window before turning in. The eerie moonlight cast shadows about the milking shed and lean-to, accentuating the vacant space usually occupied by the battered and mud-splattered car. Fiona felt a creeping sense of foreboding. Was there a message in her strange encounter with Gus earlier in the day?

Next morning after the milking was done, Michael let himself into the farmhand's room. His meagre belongings were still there – a backpack and a few items of soiled clothing heaped in a corner. He grabbed the backpack and got out in a hurry, assailed by a smell of dung and decay. He emptied the backpack on the ground and poked the contents with a stick – a crumpled dirty vest, soiled tissues, unidentifiable prescription pills and a threadbare wallet with a missing flap. Michael picked up the wallet with two fingers and found in it a long-expired driver's licence in the name of Gavin Murry.

'Oh my god,' said Fiona, her fingers trembling as she peered at the photo on the driver's licence. 'That's definitely him, our farmhand. Angus's buddy from high school days.' She slumped into a chair.

'You knew him?'

'Yeah, knew him as Gav. Don't know why he changed his name.' How strange, she thought, the way someone can become non-existent, almost vanish from one's memory, except for residues like this man's posture and movement. Nothing else.

'He must have made you out, surely? The man's not blind.' Michael flung the driver's licence onto the kitchen table. It slid and fell to the floor.

'No, not the way I am now. Flabby, good looks all gone,' she said, troubled by her husband's darkened face. Michael was not persuaded, but he did not push the point.

'Gav the guzzler' they'd called him for all the beer he drank and remained standing,' continued Fiona in a voice distant and remote. 'Met him soon after I began dating Angus. We did many things as a threesome before Angus and I married. We lost touch after his family relocated to Warragul when their house burnt down.' She went quiet knowing it made her husband uneasy on the rare occasions she mentioned her first marriage.

~

Days went by with no sign of Gus. Michael spoke

of cleaning up the lean-to in preparation for a replacement. The kids raised questions, unsettling their mother and irritating their dad. Zoe fretted that they had sent Gus away. How could they be so mean?

On impulse, Michael called on Dr Ali and explained his concern over the disappearance of his farmhand on the day the man had consulted him. 'We've no idea what happened to him. All his stuff is still as he left it. He didn't even collect his pay.'

'Hmm,' responded the doctor, elbows on the desk and hands clasped.

'Should we go to the police?'

'Look, I can't say too much. Patient confidentiality and all that, you see,' said Dr Ali. 'But to put your mind at rest, this much I can share. Your farmhand was quite ill when he came to see me. End stage lung cancer, poor fellow. Had to quit his last job as a deck hand on a container ship.'

'That's awful.'

'Don't quite understand how the man was on his feet all this while. Let alone holding a job as a farmhand.'

'So what's become of him, doctor? Where's he now?'

Dr Ali looked grave as he leaned forward across his cluttered desk, troubled that he may have already divulged far too much. 'I referred him to the Peninsular Hospice where he will receive palliative care for his remaining days.'

'You mean to die?'

Fiona's face clouded over at the news. She complained of a migraine. 'I'll lie down a bit love, if you don't mind. Could you help yourself to lunch?' Distressing thoughts gnawed at her. What's happened to me? Even if I hadn't made him out, why was I so nasty, treating him like a leper? Why? Had anger, pent up over many years blinded her? She'd been young and too naïve, believing love would somehow gild their lives with enduring certainty.

In those impressionable and carefree years, love was something magical and unreal, a gift to last. Then overnight, Angus vanished. No explanations, no forwarding address. She worried herself into weeks of insomnia, roaming the house at all hours. She was, in turn, inflamed by anger, twisted by confusion, withered with grief and overwhelmed by a sense of profound loss. She had to live with the pain of *not knowing*. Each silent day seeped into another, stretching into weeks, months and years, petrifying into an insidious longing and a loss.

A dull resignation prevailed.

Fiona sat up in bed jolted by a realisation. This is exactly how it must be for countless others who've lost loved ones: parents whose children had disappeared, never to be found; women whose sons and husbands had gone missing in war.

~

They were unusually quiet at Sunday breakfast. The plaintive mooing of cows drifted into the kitchen through the open window, interspersed with the annoying calls of crows nearby. Zoe peeked at her mother's face between bites of her sausage. 'Mum, are we allowed to visit Gus at the hospice?'

Fiona glanced at Michael.

'Yeah, let's. Dad,' Matt said. 'You can hand him his stuff then.'

'I suppose we could, but I'm not sure if he'll be well enough to receive us. Should I check, hon?

Fiona nodded with a blank look, unsure if she could handle seeing Gus again and acknowledging him. However, when Michael phoned the hospice, he was told Gus was in an induced coma and only a member of his immediate family, whom they had managed to trace, was permitted to keep vigil at his bedside. Two days later, Fiona was alone at home when Dr Ali phoned to enquire if they received news that Gus had died.

~

Who's to reason why things happen the way they do, Fiona thought as she and Zoe stood by, watching the men at work.

'Why's Dad burning Gus's things, mum?' cried Zoe as Michael and Matt, with gloved hands, cast the farmhand's paltry belongings into a pit fire behind the shed. They attended to the task in silence Flames devoured the feed like stray dogs. The family retreated as puffs of acrid smoke sought them out. A couple of cows nearby appeared indifferent to the goings on. Zoe pressed herself into Fiona, clutching her mother's embracing arms.

'Gus was a kind man, always nice to you.'

'Yes, Mum,' whispered Zoe, her eyes welling with tears.

'People die, my love, or go away never to return. What can we do but accept and say goodbye.

Fire can be so cleansing, she reflected. Much like water. They promise new life. Some memories, however, may never die but remain scattered in the ashes like imprints defining a person's life.

~

JOURNEY'S END

You go searching for the place to be
Between reality and hope,
Laughter and sorrow.
Between the push and pull
Of gravity,
The still point
In a turning world.
A distant horizon
Between sea and sky.
At journey's end
You return
Empty-handed
To where you began
And find
Equanimity.

PHOTOSHOT

It's all over the papers. *'Youth Unemployment Record High.'* I did my bit job hunting last month, didn't I? Bloody waste of time. I'd swear mum and Centrelink don't trust the papers. I suspect they're into it together. Why else would they give me a hard time? But really, I can't be bothered.

'Get up, you lazy bugger,' screams mum. 'It's near lunchtime and you're still stewing in bed.' She whisks the blanket off me like she's stripping wallpaper, exposing my privates. I cup my naked crotch and scream back.

'Leave me alone, can't ye. What's the hurry?' That sets her off nagging and threatening me, no end.

'Now, you listen to me, you useless bum. I fixed

you an interview with my boss, Mr Raffety. Get up and get there before you're disowned and end up like one of those poor buggers roughing out the nights in Flinders Street Station.

She's just about impossible to live with since Dad pissed off. Don't blame him exactly. If you know what I mean. Anyway, I go and see this bloke at Domestic Dogs R Us, Mr Raffety. He has untidy black hair: a wig, I'd swear, and he's standing in the middle of his small stuffy office leaning backward puffing away on a cigar. He reminds me of an unsafe crane on a building site.

'You say you're Mrs Pugg's boy?' I give him a glum nod. He fixes me from behind his dark glasses, grunts, explores his chin and goes silent like his stubbles remind him he's missed a shave or two.

I just stand there unnerved by his creepy silence. He finally wakes up to me.

'Try you out for a week – evenings and weekends. Casual. I don't take no shirkers, see.'

'What do I do, mister? The job I mean.'

'Check out Mrs Raffety at the back. She's the boss around here. Go through that door,' he announces gesturing over his shoulder.

'Thanks.' Honest to God, I'd rather be in bed right now.

A small bossy-looking woman with a pencil behind one ear, steps out from a cluttered and untidy office.

'What business you have drifting in here?' she quizzes, like I've come shoplifting.

'Mr Raffety sent me. I'm new.'

I keep at her heel as she shuffles about the warehouse pointing out medicines for crook and aggro dogs. Shelves and boxes of stuff – bottles of oils and watery liquids in many different colours, tubs of ointment, packets of salts, spray cans with pictures of happy dogs, and heaps of yukky-looking dried roots and herbs. Enough to give my tummy a turn. Hang in there, I say to myself as I look closely at the labels as if I can read. I finger the salts, smell the ointments and try the sprays. I must show interest and get hired else my mum will do me in.

Mrs Raffety rattles off what's for what. 'Pink oil for croup, black stinky spray for fleas, eucalyptus ointment for rash, brown salts for bad temper, green liquid for constipated and farting dogs, stuff for colic, arthritis, bad teeth and so on. I stop listening.

What a load of bull, I think. How can a bloke cram all this in his head? But I make noises like I'm impressed.

'Now, you'll carry a small supply of our products in a backpack. I'll give you a clip-board and write you a list of dog aggros and a cure for each. You'll be canvassing three streets this weekend, no more. Can you handle that?

'Yeah, but what's *canvassing?*'

'Door-knocking, boy, door-knocking,' she says in a shrill voice. 'Just the houses with *Beware of the Dog* signs, and ones where you hear a dog bark. Don't go barging in, you hear. Ring, knock or holler first for attention.'

'No problem,' I mumble. How'd I get into this shit, I think. Dogs hate my guts, I swear.

'Is there a loo around here, Missus?'

'You'll be right,' she encourages. 'Needn't get all anxious. Your mum will help you out.'

So I go on my first door-knock. Sunday afternoon. One door after another. *Knock, knock.* I adjust my cap so it's readable: *Domestic Dogs R Us!* I position myself and practise my smile should the door open. Little luck, mostly. The streets are deserted, like people have all taken off to the MCG. But this guy opens immediately like he spotted my cap from behind the curtain. Stubbie in hand. 'You'd fix a crook cur?'

'Yup, that's me job.'

He lets me into the living room.

'Your car?' I enquire spotting a photo on the mantelpiece of a mangled car.

'Yeah.'

'Quite a mess, eh? People hurt?' I ask, concerned like. But really, I'm just making conversation. No response. Just a morose look saying: What's it to you, mate? He looks away and calls over his shoulder.

'Martha, you hear me? Bloke's here that helps with dog problems.'

'I'm in the loo, see. You handle him, can't ye?'

I hear a dog at the back somewhere, barking his guts out. Maybe he got a whiff of an intruder in the house.

'But Martha, he could have something to fix Bruff!'

'Yeah! Yeah! It'll be some wait, as I'm still at it.'

So we get talking. Small talk, bloke stuff mostly. I sense he's wary. Working up to saying *Piss off now. Go see some other neighbours with cursing mongrels.* Me, I glance again at the photo on the mantelpiece – of the mangled Honda Civic. What's the story, I wonder. What's to be celebrated? Why put up with a daily reminder of a messed up prized possession? People are peculiar sometimes. Like Mum.

He picks up that my attention is back on the photo. The fellow raises his hand and takes a gulp, scratches his crotch. I'd swear he's about to fill me in on the crash when the blasted toilet gushes and gurgles like it's Christmas. Relief momentarily crosses his face, effectively flushing away whatever he had on his mind. He takes off without even a *'see ye'*. But me, I'm marooned on a bar stool, dangling me feet. Uncertain. Should I nick off now? Should I stay put? Maybe I'll strike it lucky.

I look around the room as if something there will set me on the path to *enlightenment* as my mum would say. Some hoping! No inspirational voice spills out from any nook in the room. Then, unexpected-like, a puff of alien stench hits me, almost blowing me off my perch. 'Jeesus! What the…!'

A hoarse voice enters the living room ahead of its owner, checking me out.

'You still here, you cure-all man?'

I drop off my seat in a hurry and confront the voice. There's this very large woman filling the entire hallway entrance. Martha. I greet her with a weak apologetic smile, but say nothing.

She shuffles into the room and plonks onto a well-used and ample arm-chair. It groans as the seat sinks to the floor. She catches her breath. That odour hits me again as if once is not enough. I keep my distance. What's the done thing in this situation, I wonder. I mean, for door-knocking blokes like me, just wanting to get a break in life.

It's too late to back off now and much too late to phone mum or my supervisor. I get the shakes and clutch my clip-board firmly. I pretend a smile, but Martha misses it because at that very moment she's busy rummaging in the pockets of her crumpled gown, dislodging stained tissues in the process. She pulls out her large glasses, directs her unsteady hands to her face and just about succeeds to get them on. I have time enough to size up my potential customer from head to toe and east to west. Two bleary eyes peer at me through glasses urgently needing a good clean.

'So! Whadya got to sell me, eh?'

'Have to hear you out first. My boss says I've to listen to what's messing up the customer before delivering the cure.'

'Don't give me that bullshit, boy,' she shouts. But then goes quiet like I wasn't around no more. She pulls up her morning gown above her left ankle, grimacing.

Jeesus! It's almost eaten away by an angry, weeping sore the size of a mutt's feeding bowl!

'Can't stand the blasted smell,' she complains. 'You! Don't just stand there gaping! Pass me that tray of treatment stuff. Over there on that chair,' she instructs, nodding in the direction of her gaze.

I jump to it. Hand her a messy tray with cotton wool, bandages, pins and medicine in a small bottle.

Her man drifts back into the room, drying his wet hands on his pants. 'So, youse two made a deal yet?' he asks in an indifferent voice. He hesitates, picks up the photo, inspects it, and returns it to its spot on the mantelpiece.

I fix uncomfortably on Martha's panting as she cleans and examines her ankle. I guess it's her morning routine. Can't tell if it's helping her much. I receive the finished tray respectfully from Martha and return it to the chair – my eyes and nose turned the other away.

'Have you some quick-fix stuff for a crazy dog?'

Ah! Finally, we're down to business.

'Bruff goes crazy the day my man's Honda gets crushed – parked just at the front gate! Can you believe that?' she gasps. 'Bruff's not his real name, you see. We gave it him. Maybe that makes him all mixed up! Dog trauma. That's what the vet calls it. Well, the vet's a fake. His treatment's a waste of time. Good only for galahs. Cost me a packet.

At this point the bloke butts in. 'Started me Honda 7am sharp to beat the traffic. But ducked back to collect me blasted phone. Bang! I rushed out. There, before me popping eyes, a ute has gutted me car. Hell almighty, this is calamity, I think. Hissing steam, neighbours shouting and traffic screeching all over. I run down to check. Tell ye, it was a shocker. Driver bleeding and frothing. Obvious he was a goner alright. And a crazed and cringing mutt at his side. Bloodied as well. Photo there tells it all. I'm one lucky bloke.'

Quite some speech, I think.

The bloke picks up the frame again, pours over the details as if he's seeing his mangled car for the first time. Grunts. Crosses the room and peers out the window overlooking the driveway, long and hard, as if it was all still happening.

Come on man, finish your damn story, I think. I got to get going.

'The dead man had no family to claim the poor

mutt,' Martha recollects. 'So we took him in. House was quiet as a grave, you see, since Josh, my son, took off for a mining job out west. But my neighbour's convinced we've done ourselves a mighty disservice by inheriting an unfixable mutt. Maybe she's right. Maybe he's too grief-struck for the bloke who died on him. Maybe he resents us for calling him Bruff. Not that we haven't tried to find who the mutt really was – by name I mean.'

I cross my hands and put on a sad face, but all this pretending to care stuff bothers me no end.

'What's my reward for being nice to him? A nick on me ankle. Not that he's naturally violent, you see. Just scared stiff. Troubled, like me late sister. Bless her! Panic got her good and proper. All hours of the night and day, 'til she done herself in.'

Oh yeah, it's sausage and mash night tonight, I'm thinking.

'So what'd you say? Can you help or not?'

I wake up with a thud. A hasty peek at the aggro and crook dog list on my clip board. What's the remedy? Which one is it? Confusion gets my brain turbo-charged.

When the mutt's gone crazy remembering bad stuff, don't call Ghostbusters! Call Domestic Dogs R Us. We'll deliver. For sure!

Martha's sits sullen, like a farm chook drenched in rain. 'He's a mean bastard. Sticks that picture into the mongrel's face and gets him all whimpering.

Wants to put him down, he does.' She's angry now, but also sounds helpless-like. 'He'd do it if he got the chance. Swears Bruff's a hopeless case.' There's tension creeping up the walls and sucking the air out of the room. 'Treats me no different.'

'Youse care more for that cursed mongrel than for me.' The bloke leans into the woman like the mean wolf in a kid's picture book about to jump grandma.

What am I doing here? The room spins about me. Fixing crook dogs and dousing a man-woman aggro is not my territory. Scares me stiff. I look out the window and spot a gull flying past easy as air.

'Going into hospital Monday week to fix me leg.' She wipes her eyes with the sleeve of her gown. 'I'm scared for Bruff. He's only got me to shield him.'

I spy a mess of cobwebs dangling from the ceiling in a far corner, caught in a strip of sunlight. Now that would never escape Mum's domestic eyes. No ways. Mum. That's it. She's the answer. Why hadn't I thought of that before?

'I've various stuff here in my backpack for most dog problems - oils, ointments, drinks. But your Bruff is a special case. Serious-like. Needs special professional treatment, see? Mind if I step out for a minute to consult my supervisor?'

'Suit yourself,' says Martha 'but get a-move on, as I'm called to the loo again'

I scramble for my mobile. 'Mum, Mum! You got to help me. I'm in a fix!'

'Slow down, son. You in trouble again?'

I blurt out my predicament, but Mum's not persuaded.

'Walk a nice friendly dog for a week or so, you say, while your customer is in hospital? Is that it? You sure?'

'Yes,' I plead. 'Bruff's being sorely harassed by the bloke in the house. A dog hater.'

'What, you mean you haven't made a sale yet?'

'It's complicated, Mum. The man and woman need fixing first.'

'You hopeless nitwit, I'll save your skin this time. Not ever again. Tell Martha I'm on the way.'

'Thanks, Mum. I'll pay you back. Promise.' My relief is like when I've done a mighty big pee.

'Don't bother, son. I swear, I knew you'd muck up.'

I hurry back before the bloke comes snooping. 'Consulted my boss on the phone, Martha. Good news for you. I've arranged a professional dog protector for Bruff for the time you're in hospital.'

'You're sure?' she asks in a hesitant voice.

'Very professional woman. Simply loves dogs. She's on her way now to meet you and get acquainted with Bruff – with your help, of course.'

A weary smile crosses Martha's face.

'Give the young man a stubbie, will ye,' she

orders.

But the bloke grunts, gives her the finger and takes off. Good riddance, I think. That's the last I'll see of him.

'Guess I'll move on then, if you don't mind. Check out a few more houses on your street while the day lasts.'

Martha gathers herself with effort and lumbers off the way she'd come, like a sickly elephant heading for a water-hole. But the bad smell decides to keep me company.

~

As I make for the front door, the framed wreck gives me the evil eye. I bolt. Stumble into empty stubbies on the landing. The crashing din sets off a frenzy of barking! Enough to wake up bad folks in hell.

'What's the hurry, mate?' A mocking voice calls from the shadow of the carport. Bruff is straining on his leash, choking and snarling at the same time.

I freeze.

'Scared the mean beast will nick your butt? Ha, Ha!'

'Stuff ye!' I mutter as I scuttle off. A real shit of a job this is.

He lets go of Bruff. The bugger comes hurtling towards me and knocks me clean over.

I'm a goner, I scream in my head, done in by a crazy mutt. My clipboard takes off without me as I hit the dirt. Liquid stuff from my backpack spills onto me.

I come to. There's an awful smell and goo all over my face. 'Get off me,' I shout, trying to push away the mutt who is determined to lick the very skin off me face.

'Jake, stop mucking about this very minute.' It's my miracle Mum to the rescue.

'Get moving now. Had to tell Mr Raffety you're in a fix. I feel so ashamed.'

Martha peers from behind a window on the far side, her face like bad weather.

~

VIRTUAL PEOPLE

We are but two virtual people
From years gone by,
Far too many to
Contemplate.
We are but two virtual people,
Unreal,
Without form
Without voice.
Distant memories.
Drifting blobs of consciousness
Flitting back and forth
Between two ends of an
Electronic trail;
Miracle of a kind.

SPIRITUAL PLAY

My mother named me Maya, the heavenly one. But I'm the one still earth-bound, while Mum and Dad and the best of my violin pupils have all been spirited away. I lie awake, night after night, with my lonely thoughts flitting about in the dark, ferreting ancient memories. Despite the years, I still feel the strings of my violin flutter and sing, still hear the cadence deep within me. Blighted with age and infirmity, all I can do now is embrace my rare instrument and recall how it came into my possession. A truly strange and remarkable story, you'll soon agree.

~

I first laid eyes on the stranger about fifty years ago when I was attending a violin recital in Melbourne with a friend. I was an impressionable twenty-two then, having graduated from the Royal Academy of Music in London. We couldn't get seats together, so my friend sat diagonally behind me. We had much to chat about while waiting for the concert to begin. Each time I turned to speak with her, I couldn't help but notice the woman next to her. She was lean-faced, remote and infinitely wise-looking with an iconic mop of bleached hair. She reminded me of Einstein. We exchanged a tentative smile but never spoke. Carefree and young, my friend and I chatted and laughed, indifferent to others encircling us. Much like the countless strangers that flit across my everyday life, I didn't think of the woman again.

A year later, I participated as a violinist in an Amnesty International charity concert in Adelaide, which included a three-course dinner. I stood at the auditorium door with other musicians welcoming guests, while ushers checked their tickets. It was a wintry evening, and I shivered each time someone let in a chill blast of air as they entered the foyer. Then a woman in a long overcoat pushed through the double doors and held them open, lingering as if unsure she'd come to the right event. Come on, make up your mind, I thought as I drew my jacket tightly around me and pulled up my collar. As she made her way towards me, I had one of those rare moments of instant recognition. But where had I seen that distinguished mop of unruly hair before?

'My ticket,' I overheard the woman say to an usher in a strong foreign accent. Then she acknowledged my presence.

'Feeling zee cold, yah? You poor girl.' Her smile was amused, yet sympathetic.

I glanced quickly at her face as she removed her overcoat, but still couldn't place her.

'Your friend, how eez she?'

'Ma'am?'

Her eyes sparkled. 'Ah, you don't know me? The violin recital in Milbourn, remember? Last November. Your friend sat near me.'

Amazingly, I could see the moment, full and complete, as if it just happened. I even remembered her pearl necklace. Before I could recover my composure, she disappeared into the auditorium with grace and dignity. It surprised me how slender and tall she appeared.

I joined the musicians assembled on stage, tuning their instruments, positioning microphones, gesturing and whispering. That night I played the lead violin in a quartet. We had chosen Pachelbel's Canon in D. On the final note, the audience gave us a rousing applause. My heart filled with pride.

After the performance, as I joined Mum and Dad in the auditorium for dinner, Mum whispered, 'Darling, say hello to Mrs Goltz. She's excited to speak with you.'

And there next to me sat the mystery woman.

'Why, hello,' I said. 'What a coincidence. At least now I know your name.'

'Mrs Goltz says she'd seen you before, Maya. She's amazed you are such an accomplished violinist,' said Mum, bright-eyed.

'Why are you surprised?' I said turning to Mrs Goltz as I took my seat.

'Vell for a start your fiolin blaying is enchanting, dear. Quite spirited.'

I laughed.

'The thing is, Maya,' said Mrs Goltz, leaning over and speaking into my ear above the noise. 'I've been looking for a fiolinist for an event I'm organising next month. But not just any fiolinist, you see.'

She read my puzzled look.

'I have an offer for you, young lady,' she added with a wink and a reassuring touch of my shoulder. 'Here's my card. You call me in a few days, yah?'

I felt flattered and intrigued.

Mum and Dad smiled with evident delight.

~

For some reason, I felt uneasy about Mrs Goltz and her offer. But after a week of Mum's relentless persuasion, I gave in. Dad drove me to see Mrs Goltz. She lived in a weatherboard house in the Adelaide Hills, its facade almost hidden by a rambling bougainvillea bush in extravagant bloom. She opened the front door as soon as I rang, as if she couldn't wait.

'Come in, my dear, come in,' said my beaming host, her casually worn string of pearls dancing with glee. A mottled green parrot perched on her shoulder. 'Hello, yah. Hello yah,' it chirped repeatedly in Mrs Goltz's voice. A swell of birdcalls came from remote parts of the house. A large ginger cat silently nudged at my ankle. I was embraced and ushered to a back patio where a coffee table was set for tea. We sat in wicker chairs. I looked around but could see no birdcages.

'Don't mind my little ones,' said Mrs Goltz as she shut the patio door. 'They'll quieten down soon. Just excited by your visit. I'll show you my aviary later if you vish.' The cat jumped onto my lap but slunk away when scolded. We made some small talk while she served tea.

'Here, look at this invitation and this book, Maya. You see, I vill launch a biography of my late husband written by me. Years of hard work. You vill blay for us, yah? Beethoven's Fiolin Sonata No 9 in A Major vich my husband simply adored.'

I protested that, at such short notice, I may not be able to meet her expectation. However, it made no difference. She was either a woman determined to have her own way or was simply hard of hearing.

'You vill blay the Beethoven on the fiolin I give you. Vait I show you.' She disappeared and returned promptly with a violin, which looked to be quite ancient. 'See, I vill gift you this fiolin to safe-keep like your only child. But you must blay only this all the time, yah?'

In the family of violins, there's none as rare and precious as a Stradivarius. I was blown away to be presented with one. Her words rang in my head. I reached for a glass of water.

~

I was pleased with myself for surviving the book launch. I received smiles and applause for my playing. But in truth it was Mrs Goltz's magic violin that rose to the occasion.

~

Several weeks later, I met Mrs Goltz in a city centre cafe. She had vital information for me, she said. It was only then I learned that the violin, in fact, was not her husband's. But what followed unsettled me more.

'I've been looking for you for thirty years, my dear. My husband bleaded I find a vorthy custodian to keep alive the spirit of this fiolin. And now he vill rest happy.'

'But I don't understand, Mrs Goltz. If your husband wasn't the owner, who was? And, are you telling me to play this violin and no other for the rest of my life?' A headache was coming on.

'Ven my husband was still an unmarried young man, he lived with his mother in a small farming town not too far from Stuttgart. The local military ordered him to use his farm truck to transport families evicted from their homes to the railway station. Yah, he soon guessed vat vas happening. They ended up in internment camps. My husband vas a kind man. It upset him to see the fear in the faces of these people among whom he had lived all his life. He knew many by name.'

As I listened, the lunch-hour traffic outside the café suddenly appeared dream-like, unstable and illusory. She continued in earnest.

'He had to be careful to say or do nothing, you see, fearing that he and his family may be accused and bunished as sympathisers and collaborators. It vas troubling times even before the war, my dear. My husband vas courteous and gentle vith the elderly, the vomen and small children. He helped them onto his farm truck with their little belongings, always under the vaching eyes of the Gestapo.'

Mrs Goltz paused, her eyes glazing over. 'I guess you voudn't know much about Hitler and the nasty var? Believe me it vas very bad. Very bad.'

It's true I had only remote impressions of the war, gleaned mostly from American movies.

'In any case, how you say, *to cut the string short* this is how my husband got the fiolin.'

'I still don't get it,' I said.

'Didn't I say someone left it behind in the back of his truck? Vell my husband said he found the fiolin wrapped in a man's winter coat with a quickly written note. He was cleaning the truck after a long upsetting day. Let me see now, I think it said something like *I bray someone give this fiolin a safe home. My father and grandmother loved blaying it. I too. You must blay and enjoy. Dinah Altdorf.*

'Oh my god, that's awful,' I said, rubbing my temple.

'He told me nothing, my husband, even though I vas his wife for forty years. I only got to know the truth ven the doctor said he had cancer and vee had to move to a retirement unit. Ve can't take all our stuff with us, I told him quite firmly. And this fiolin just sitting here. You never blay it. So vy don't ve give it to someone who vill use it? He gasped and spluttered. It shocked me how angry he got. It really did. Only then did he tell me everything. He vas still heavy vith guilt, you see, believing he somehow caused the death of many people from his town, including the family who belonged to the fiolin.'

It was all beginning to make sense. Needing air, I pushed my chair back and stood up.

Mrs Goltz frowned. 'You've not finished your coffee, my dear.'

'I'm a little late getting home,' I said, wishing Mum hadn't pushed me into helping Mrs Goltz.

~

For more than a year I couldn't touch the violin. I couldn't shake off the thought that it was haunted. I had nightmares of people dying, and loud wails coming from the violin when I'd played it the first few times. I shoved the case into a cupboard in the spare room, among other junk.

The turning point came unexpectedly one morning when Dad returned from his morning walk with a copy of the *Adelaide Advertiser*. 'Read this,' he said pointing to a brief article at the bottom of the front page.

Farm truck hit and kills elderly German woman at a pedestrian crossing.

'Oh no, it can't be,' I said clutching the paper. I was shattered. Not only had I promised to keep in touch with Mrs Goltz, but had given her a solemn undertaking not to treat her violin as a museum piece. But this was exactly what I'd done. I'd packed it away.

'Come now, don't be hard on yourself,' said Mum. 'The best medicine for you is to play at her wake. Go on, phone her family.'

What an unreasonable suggestion, I thought. But I plucked up enough courage to retrieve the violin from storage. The moment I held it, I felt a shiver wash through my body, the very experience that had unnerved me years earlier. Not again, I resolved. I'll not be undone.

I recall Mum accompanying me to the wake, which was a modest and dignified event. About thirty people were present, mostly grey-haired, with solemn faces contemplating mortality. Following the eulogy in German, I was invited to the front and introduced simply as a talented violinist and a benefactor of Mrs Goltz's generosity. The mourners fixed their eyes on me with intense curiosity. I was by far the youngest in the room and also of a very different cultural background. My palms perspired.

Mum whispered, 'Play, love, play. They're waiting.'

Almost miraculously, my Stradivarius came alive with a rendering of Pachelbel's Canon in D. I simply followed. I breathed easily as the bow slid effortlessly over the strings. The music ebbed and flowed, filling the hall and uplifting the hearts of all present.

Mum was right. Playing at the wake was therapeutic. It helped me shed my irrational fear. Thereafter, this violin never left my side as I travelled the world and performed countless times. The spirits of all those faceless people who once owned my Stradivarius, and had enjoyed its magic, remained with me over the years.

But that time is now spent. The spirits have departed. Shrouded in dark silence and captive to a flood of memories, I lie awake. The nights seem to last forever. A dog barks in the distance. I turn on my side and surrender to a spate of yawning.

~

SURVIVING SADNESS

When a flood of sadness
Washes over you
Drawing you under
Gasping for air,
Ask
How you may endure
If not with wisdom and
A pocket full of
Courage?

A RECONCILIATION MYTH

The eyes of the whole class followed the teacher's hand as he wrote on the board. *Everyone agreed that the day was just right for the picnic at Hanging Rock.*[1] Now who can guess where that famous line comes from?' Mr Logan said with an expectant glance around the class. It was once again creative writing hour for year 10 at Mount Macedon High School.

Two hands shot up, one tentative. A few students shuffled and looked away, not wanting to be called upon.

'Well Ron?'

'From over there, Mr Logan.' Ron pointed out

[1] Line from *Picnic at Hanging Rock*, Joan Lindsey

the window across the hazy, winter landscape. 'Hanging Rock, Sir. Me and my family had a BBQ there on New Year's Day. Mum and Dad bet on horses.'

Muffled giggles disturbed the class like rustling leaves in a passing breeze.

'Quite right. You've reminded us that there's horse racing at Hanging Rock to mark New Year and Australia Day. Class, if you fix your eyes out there through the window, you'll see an outcrop of jagged, volcanic rocks. Barely visible in this miserable weather. Has anyone here explored Hanging Rock?'

Keen students called out, 'me, me, Mr Logan.'

'My Mum saw a movie about girls gone missing ages ago at Hanging Rock,' said Nadia above the chatter.

'Fake news, fake news,' Tom said. 'The Weekend Australian said so last week. My grandpa was telling Dad at dinner about this article he had read, which said the indigenous folks in Mount Macedon were upset by that story. They've launched the *Miranda Must Go campaign*.'

'Yeah,' mumbled Nullah.

'What's that, Nullah? Please speak up.'

'Bin to the Rock with me Auntie Mavis last summer. Read the story board there behind the tourist information office, Mr Logan. All about the picnic and them girls who got lost. Happened fifty years ago. But Auntie says it's a load of bull and the made-up story just messes up the real history.'

'Can you please explain to the class what Hanging Rock means to the Kulin nation?'

'Well, I dunno much, Sir, except my mob, the Dja Dja Wurrung, called it Nyannelong. Long before white people come, it was a place for secret men's business, like initiation ceremonies.

This elicited puzzled and questioning looks, appeals to Mr Logan to rescue the situation, to offer clarity on what was now turning into a touchy matter.

'That's it in a nutshell, class,' said Mr Logan skirting the issue. He explained that Joan Lindsey's 1967 novel *Picnic at Hanging Rock* told of a group of white school girls on a picnic outing in which a couple of them, together with a teacher, go exploring the rocky outcrop and never return. This happened on 14 February 1900, Valentine's Day. The novel was made into a film, which is now considered an Australian classic. A mystery has since formed around the story. Some say it's pure fiction, but others claim it's based on fact.

'But Nullah is also correct. The local Aboriginal people do wish to reclaim Hanging Rock and promote its sacred heritage.'

'What's the assessment task, Mr Logan? You've not told us.'

'Quite correct, Martha. Let me explain. There'll

be two parts to the writing project. Firstly, to help you understand the background, we will watch the Hanging Rock film together during our next double English lesson. Note the date in your diary. Then, you will each study a short piece of fiction I will give you and write your impressions of it. Is this clear?'

Total silence.

'No need to sweat on it,' Mr Logan smiled, sensing apprehension in the air. 'You've studied the basics of creative writing in our previous classes. Here's another opportunity to apply your skills.'

Someone from the back said, 'the reading stuff, Mr Logan, is it difficult?'

'Not difficult at all. I've simply made up a different version of what could have happened to Miranda, the main character in the story. I call it *A Reconciliation Myth*. In your feedback, pay particular attention to the ending. Is it appropriate, or should the story have concluded in some other way?'

Nullah put up his hand, and Mr Logan nodded.

'Sir, I don't think we can manage that. I mean find fault with what you write.'

'Not to worry. You'll do well. Just apply what you've learnt and be bold about it.'

~

As promised, Mr Logan produced the following piece of writing for the class to critique:

While everyone was preoccupied, Miranda, always the

dreamer, slipped away unnoticed from the picnic spot. She picked her way through a stretch of tall buffalo grass, the colour of wheat. If someone stopped her, she thought, she'd say she was only following the bees and butterflies to the lively creek close by. But the truth was that the moment she left the carriage, she felt driven by a certainty that destiny was close at hand. Hadn't her mysterious Valentine's Day card promised as much? She was dressed in a flowing white long-sleeved dress fringed with lace. Her flaxen hair, modestly plaited, glowed. Miranda looked every bit a rose about to open itself to possibilities.

She followed a narrow path through fern and grass, crossed a shallow creek stepping over stones and headed towards rocky outcrops just visible through the trees. The path became steeper. Up and up went Miranda. She had the feeling she was the only person alive. The sun whirled and whirled from a cloudless sky. The air was heavy with the smell of eucalyptus. She faltered in the heat and dense haze. Her chest heaved. Her mouth was dry as ash. She sat on a fallen log, discarded her boots, peeled off her gloves and stockings and shook her hair loose.

Miranda climbed higher and entered an unfamiliar world – a moonscape of jagged conical outcrops, caves, sudden passageways, deep pits, precarious boulders, columns of rock, and unexpected courtyards. She scrambled onto a rocky platform to see how much further she had to go, certain she'd know when she arrived. A flock of screeching parrots flew past. A little way to her right soared a monolith, dark against the light. This overbearing Rock was pockmarked, fissured and scarred by lichen. As she shielded her eyes and gazed fixedly at the Rock, Miranda believed she saw the gaunt and age-weary face of an old man. Was he the keeper of Hanging Rock? She felt strangely drawn towards it.

It was high noon. The heat was relentless. Every cell in her body cried to be quenched. Indifferent to their plea, Miranda persisted, propelled by a purpose now beyond understanding. It seemed her thoughts, feelings and senses were dissolving and reforming, dissolving and reforming like clouds in urgent flight. Even the world around her was no longer stable or certain. Shadow and light melded with images of landscape – sky and earth, rock and trees, insects and birds. Ah yes, I'm free-floating in a dream-world, she thought.

Miranda felt as if she had been travelling a long while, almost years. But the distance was covered in accelerated time. Even the sun, unhinged from its zenith, had crossed the sky and arrived in the western horizon, resting a little behind the massive rock-face, which now cast deepening shadows across a confined open space. It was almost twilight.

Miranda knew she had arrived in a special and privileged space. Dizzy from exertion and overwhelmed by the moment, she lowered herself onto her knees. She raised her eyes to the monolith but was blinded by light from the setting sun. No sooner had the sun slipped fully behind the Rock than the its scarred and inscrutable face emerged from the gloom, enormous and majestic. Miranda was transfixed. Her heart raced. As she gazed unblinking upon the Rock, it seemed to shift and take life.

A human figure formed. It stepped out. It was a young man, no older than Miranda but much taller. His naked body was sinewy and taut and glistened a chocolate-purple. His face was broad. He was endowed with well-formed teeth, large bright eyes set in deep sockets, a broad nose, and a mop of soot-black hair. He smiled as if pleased to be set free. The face was remarkably similar to a youthful version of the Rock. He took a few tentative steps towards Miranda. For a moment, he stood on one leg, supported at the knee by the sole of the other. The young man made cracking sounds with his clapsticks. Miranda, mesmerised, did not stir. She did not doubt this was a fully grown young man, unashamedly displaying his manhood. But she hadn't seen anyone like him before, not even in picture books. A strange warmth welled up in her, consuming her heart and mind. Her cheeks burned. It was altogether a strange new feeling. She felt an urge to rise and touch him.

The young man circled her a few times, studying Miranda. Suddenly he jumped back and uttered excited sounds in a strange tongue. He leaned into Miranda's face and fired rapid questions, pointing to her breasts. She froze. The next moment, he threw down his clapsticks and ran off.

The light was fading fast. The air was cooler now, more bearable. A pale moon was becoming brighter. Miranda was intoxicated with weariness and wonder. She fell back on her haunches and closed her eyes.

A rustling sound disturbed her. The young man had returned looking very different. White clay covered his face, except for circles exposing his eyes, mouth and nose.

Horizontal stripes of yellow and red ochre crossed his chest and upper arms and white dots ran down his lower arms. He assumed a crouching posture with his hands up at the elbows, each clutching a sprig of speckled yellow-white flowers. His eyes, deceptively larger than before, danced from side to side. Still crouching, he stomped in deliberate steps towards Miranda and back, then side to side, and every now and then circled her—as if he was imitating the courtship dance of a lyrebird. It was hypnotic. Miranda soon found her consciousness drifting into a cloud.

Darkness gave way to the yellow light of dawn. The Rock glistened with dew. Stillness prevailed. Her purpose spent, Miranda sat propped up at its base, bare feet stretched out in front. From a little distance, it seemed as if she was fast asleep, folded in the embrace of the monlith's deep shadow. Strands of her tangled locks fluttered now and again, as a gentle breeze passed by. Her hands rested on her lap, lightly touching two wilting sprigs of speckled yellow-white flowers. A mottled butterfly flitting uncertainly in the air hovered for a moment over the flowers only to be scared off by a pair of curious honey-eaters, which landed at Miranda's feet. They chirped and hopped about looking for feed, even pecking at the flowers on her lap. A monitor lizard emerged from the shadow and lifted his head to sunlight but scurried away when he sensed an approaching threat.

Miranda did not hear the urgent calling of her name 'Miraaanda, Miraaanda' from the picnic grounds far below, nor the yelping of dogs. Her face, soiled and sunburnt from relentless heat and exertion, was serene. The sounds of men and dogs echoed and echoed, only to be lost in the empty spaces and crevices all around.

~

Mr Logan was impressed with his students' varied responses and complimented them unreservedly. There was a spontaneous ripple of nods and smiles.

'I couldn't tell if Miranda lived or died,' said Bruno at the back of class.

'Of course, she died, silly,' said Sylvia. 'That's why she didn't hear the search party calling her. And why else would birds hop all over her without fear?'

Now that Sylvia has settled that matter,' said Mr Logan, 'let's discuss your comments on how I ended my version of the story. It interests me that hardly anyone seemed happy with it. Instead you've come up with contrasting and original ideas. Let's get some representative examples.'

With this Mr Logan called on three students to speak their mind in front of the class based on their written comments.

Martha said the ending upset her. 'Miranda was a foolish girl. She took off on her own without water and a hat. Got into strife and lost her mind. She should have known the summer heat was a killer. I'd have felt so much better if the search party had found her dying but still managed to save her.'

'Yeah, yeah,' shouted a few students in unison. Others clapped.

Mr Logan thanked Martha for her confidence.

'Now, Nullah, you think otherwise, don't you?'

Nullah's shoulders slumped. 'Can I just read what I've written rather than talk, Mr Logan?'

'Certainly, but from next to me, facing the class, so your voice carries.'

'I know why Miranda got into strife, Mr Logan. She shouldn't have gone to that place. And not taken up with that young blackfella.' Nullah raised his head, gazed in the direction of the window where the sun shone from a clear sky. 'But I also feel sorry it happened this way.' With that he hastened to his seat.

Except for some paper shuffling and a cough or two, there was silence. Those closest to the window looked out. Dark and craggy outcrops stood out over a canopy of stringy-bark and blackwood trees.

'We've listened to two divergent views,' said Mr Logan. 'But a small but significant number of you suggested an ending you considered more satisfying. Nadia reflects this third view.'

Nadia sauntered to the front, tossing her dark plaits behind her. The boys clapped and cheered until they were scolded.

'Well, we all know about Valentine's Day and all that stuff,' said Nadia. 'I think Miranda went out looking for her perfect boyfriend, and somehow got carried away.' This comment raised snide remarks, whispers and cat-calls. Nadia stopped and gave the class her middle finger.

‘Come now, quieten down and listen respectfully. Give Nadia a chance to finish. And Nadia, what you just did was rude and quite unnecessary.’

‘I think Miranda found who she was looking for. The black guy who danced before her, all made up. I think true love is everything. It should be a winner every time.’

‘But what about the ending, Nadia? What’s your suggestion?’

‘Sir, the best thing that could happen is for the two to escape deep in the night, escape from Hanging Rock into the valley below. Come morning, we see the two walking, hand in hand, over the open grassland, making for the nearest waterhole where they find an Aboriginal camp. They make their home there and enjoy good times.’

The students erupted into a wave of cheering and clapping, confirming the prevailing sentiment of the class. Unnoticed at the rear of the room, Nullah remained still, his hands resting quietly on the desk in front of him.

~

HOME BREW

If you must insist
Black tea will do.
Not that stuff
Youse call Earl Grey;
That's not a brew for a fella
Like me.
But me wife's fancy like,
She's for Lady Grey
All the way.
I sip at her cup
Accidentally,
Splutter all over her
And land meself
In serious strife
With my missus

Mad as hell.
Bugger me, I say
Better quit
Drinking tea
Altogether
And take to more respectable stuff
Like genuine brew for blokes.

HAZARDS OF SNOOPING

It was his father who instilled in him a lifelong wariness of authority – especially the uniformed gun-toting kind. His bedtime stories were of him serving in the South Vietnamese army, his capture and harsh treatment in the hands of the Viet Cong supported by Communist China.

'Keep away, son. Be guarded always.' So Phong was least prepared for the kind of text he received from his wife, mid-morning.

What you've been up to Phong? Why've the police stopped me at kinder? Phone me.'

He phoned immediately. 'What's happened?'

'Sergeant Andrew Lee wants to see the owner of our car ASAP. You're just like the kids, can't keep out of trouble.'

Shit! What could the police want with me? he thought, suppressing a shudder. He got up abruptly from his desk and left the building for a smoke. His mind was awhirl with frightening scenarios. What if he was held for questioning, even tortured? On the other hand, it could be a case of mistaken identity. At tea break, he left work on the pretext of having a migraine.

In no time, he was at Springvale police station. The reception desk was unattended. The waiting area was large and foreboding with only a couple of plastic chairs against a wall. Phong suspected his arrival had already been noted by hidden cameras. A clean-shaven young constable dressed in police-issue blue shirt and dark pants appeared from a door behind reception. His identity badge read Constable Wilson. Phong explained the reason for his visit.

'Take a seat. Detective Sergeant Lee is on a call.'

Phong stood fiddling with his car keys. I should have had a pee, he thought. Too late now.

The constable reappeared and beckoned, 'The detective will see you now. Follow me.'

Phong was ushered past a clutter of open plan work areas, vacant at this hour, and deposited in a cramped office with a desk and two bucket chairs. Apart from two neglected coffee mugs with a curious fly resting on one, a computer and tray with bloated manila folders occupied the desk. The room smelt of sweet-and-sour pork.

I can't handle this, thought Phong. His mouth felt dry. A squat, almost bald Asian man with a generous paunch entered and plonked himself behind the desk.

'Sit. I'm Detective Sergeant to you.' He wore jeans and a black jacket, which he removed and flung on the back of his chair. The collar of his grey polo shirt was frayed.

Phong sat on the edge of his chair.

'Let's get down to business,' said Lee. He retrieved something from a manila folder and thrust it across to Phong.

'Take a look. Tell me it's not you in the photo.'

The identity was all too obvious. It can't be, thought Phong with mounting alarm. But it was him in the photo, standing beside his car and talking to an Islander man in front of a derelict house. Who would have taken it? Clearly he'd been spied on. He couldn't believe such things happened in Australia.

'I did nothing wrong,' he blurted, mustering courage. 'Why am I here? I have rights, you know.'

'Listen here,' Lee snapped, leaning forward with elbows planted on the desk, 'if you've read the papers you'll know we are investigating a serious crime at that house you visited. Consider yourself the one and only person of interest. Take my advice and come clean or else. With that he flung a copy of the Springvale Leader at Phong. The headlines read:

Woman dies in suspicious circumstances. Son bashed to death.

'It seems you're somehow implicated, my friend. Now explain yourself. And no bull-shitting.'

Phong wedged his hands between his thighs. His bladder cried for relief. God, I wish I hadn't foolishly gone snooping around, he thought. He remembered his late father's caution to keep a distance from authority. It was obvious that the incriminating photo was taken when he went to see Rosalyn, his mother's loyal Mauritian friend. His mother had died suddenly of a heart attack a month earlier. She had been a chronic hoarder since escaping great scarcity and deprivation in Vietnam, and had taken to collecting trash and treasure from various places - including unwanted bags from this generous friend Rosalyn. While sorting out and disposing of the stuff, Phong stumbled upon an intriguing note, hand-scrawled on discoloured wrapping paper. What's this? he'd thought as he read the message aloud.

Help Danger Help Me Please.

On impulse, Phong detoured to Rosalyn's house while shopping in Springvale – even though he had promised his wife not to obsess over the note. He also puzzled why Rosalyn had not come to the funeral. It was, therefore, natural that he visits Rosalyn to see if she was okay and to thank her for having been his mother's enduring friend. However, he was aware, too, of being driven by a foolish curiosity. It was silly to think she was in real danger. A simple explanation from her would suffice.

Scanning the weatherboard house from the nature strip, he couldn't see any sign of life. It appeared abandoned with rotted guttering and clumps of bluish-green lichen covering the roof tiles. The narrow front yard was overgrown with yellowing weeds, which even encroached onto the pavement. Make-shift curtains hung in the front windows. Phong wondered if he should knock on the door. Just then a battered blue ute pulled into the driveway next door. A large man eased himself out. Phong, feeling suddenly uncertain, was about to jump into his car and take off when the man called out.

'What's up, mate?' The man waddled up in thongs.

'Just looking,' said Phong attempting to conceal his anxiety. He noticed that the unfenced house diagonally opposite was partially burnt and seemed uninhabited. A gutted truck with a rear cabin stood nearby, the cabin doors ajar, revealing a load of junk.

'Yeah?'

'The owner, she's not in?'

'If you mean the lady who lived there, she left two weeks back. Sudden like.' Close up, the man was heavy-set and rough, unshaven, with a large head defined by unruly hair. He wore oversized knee-length Bermuda shorts and a faded vest just about covering his paunch, his belly-button quite in evidence. Tattoos of various hues graced his upper right arm and one side of his muscular neck. Discoloured teeth completed the picture.

'Anyways, whose you to ask, eh?'

The man moved even closer, breathing into Phong's face. He smelt of marijuana and piss. Just then the wind picked up, herding dead leaves on the street and scattering them about.

Phong unlocked his car in haste. 'Thanks, but I must be leaving.'

'Ya haven't said what you doing here, mate.' He pushed back strands of matted hair off his forehead and glared.

Phong considered some explanation to justify his presence. 'The woman Rosalyn was my late mother's friend. Wasn't at the funeral. Just came to thank her.'

'Bugger off, now,' said the man with menace. 'Don't let me catch ya snooping around again.' With that he waddled back to his ute, his Bermuda shorts clinging to his ample buttocks.

~

Detective Lee pinned his quarry with an unrelenting stare. 'Say you're involved or you'll be my guest tonight. Get it?

Phong felt the heat. With no way out, he

confessed how he had found the cryptic SOS message among Rosalyn's stuff and how he attempted to uncover its mystery.

Unconvinced, Detective Lee fired back. 'So why did you not report it to the police? Why go poking around? Consider yourself a smart arse private eye or something, eh?'

'I was silly I know,' Phong pleaded. 'I didn't mean to do your job Mr Lee, Sir.'

'Detective Sergeant, if you don't mind,' said Lee sharply.

Phong was relieved when a police officer opened the office door without knocking and thrust her head in.

'Sorry Lee, the boys are grabbing themselves coffee. What can I get ya?'

'Thanks Joanne, a doughnut and cappuccino. Four sugars, please.' He handed her a ten dollar note and then turned his attention back to Phong.

'That Islander bloke in the picture – what you and him been up to? How come he's taken off?'

'Nothing, I swear. I hadn't seen the man before in my life.'

'Don't play the innocent Vietnamese game with me. The Americans will not rescue you this time.' Detective Lee stood up and checked his watch. He could do with a drink. But then sat abruptly, startling Phong who was caught up in fearful thoughts.

‘What can you tell me about an Asian crime syndicate operating at Crown?’

Phong crossed his arms instinctively to conceal his dank armpits. ‘What crime syndicate?’

‘Small fry hoping for a piece of the action, eh? Isn’t that it?’

Phong felt dizzy.

Detective Lee was in his element. ‘Yeah, a piece of the action. That’s exactly what the Mauritian bloke went for,’ he ranted. ‘The dumb bouncer at Crown, I suspect, thought he’d double-cross the Chinese mafia. Swiped their laundered cache and, to top it all off, used his poor mother as cover. But they stuffed him good and proper. And his mother.’

Phong sat frozen, his bladder no longer under control. He had strayed into the territory of organised crime. Stuck his stupid finger into a hornet’s nest. What was to become of him?

The detective fingered his stubbled chin in silence. The lone fly, bored with sitting on the coffee mug, flew in circles above Phong. ‘I have two battered corpses in the freezer,’ he said as if he was sharing a confidence. ‘And you’re likely to join them soon, my friend, if the thugs get you.’

‘But why?’

‘Stands to reason. If the Islander, a buddy of the deceased Mauritian, is also dead or has taken off with vital information, then you’re the only one still alive who knows where the cache is hidden.’

Phong jumped up, knocking over his chair. He clutched at his hair and broke into hysterical sobs, pleading in Vietnamese. I don't know about any stolen money.'

Detective Sergeant Lee got up with a satisfied grin, his hands on his ample waist. A gentle knock on the door distracted him.

'This bloke's wife and little ones come to collect him, Sarge,' announced the clean-shaven constable.

'I'll let you off Phong for now. But first, the Constable will take your statement. Make sure you produce the SOS note – to back up your story. If you ask me, I'd say you concocted the whole thing.'

Phong blew his nose, feeling shaken and feverish. His wet pants clung to his thighs.

'And another thing,' said Detective Lee coming over to Phong. 'You will meet me tomorrow at ten sharp at Rosalyn's house. Be ready to point out where the money's hidden. Understand? Ten sharp.'

~

'You're in no state to go anywhere,' frowned Phong's wife the next morning. 'I'll phone your work and get you to the doctor.'

'No, no. What about the police?' Phong fretted and paced the floor.

'You're a sorry mess,' she said her face a mixture of concern and frustration. 'Can't see why the police would think you could help them.'

'Detective Sergeant Lee. He instructed I meet

him this morning. He'll probably jail me if I don't.'

'Go back to bed, Phong. I'll phone the doctor as soon as I've sorted out the kids.'

One of the mobile phones charging in the kitchen rang. It was Phong's. His wife answered.

'Who's that? Oh, but my husband's quite unwell. Yeah but…'

'Is it for me?' said Phong from the bedroom.

'You'll send a police car… and I can accompany him? Okay then.'

Phong was at her side as she rang off. 'Was it Detective Sergeant Lee? Who's sending a car?'

'Detective Gomez, a woman detective will meet us.'

'Why?' said Phong in disbelief, still smarting from the grilling the previous day.

'I'm told your Lee is away on unexpected leave. I suppose on full pay.'

I hope he rots in hell, thought Phong.

~

Phong stood in front of Rosalyn's house for the second time. He felt queasy as he leaned on his wife's arm.

'Well, where should we start, Phong?' said Detective Gomez, a slight woman with an open countenance and piercing eyes. She was dressed in a police-issue blue slacks and jacket. Three other police stood by, a sniffer dog for assistance. Curious onlookers emerged from nowhere. Failing to get a response from Phong, Gomez instructed her men to begin searching the house and grounds.

'My husband can't help,' intervened Phong's wife. 'He has nothing to do with the crime.'

Detective Gomez gave an ambiguous nod and went to join the police at work, but returned when their effort proved fruitless.

'Unless you help us, we'll get nowhere,' she said pointedly to Phong, disregarding his wife's earlier plea.

Under mounting pressure, Phong wracked his brain, recalling a few of the crime stories he'd seen on TV. He spoke to his wife in Vietnamese, appealing to her for ideas to placate the police. An elderly woman spectator with a child in a stroller elbowed him and whispered with interest, 'Are you after the reward?'

'Huh? What reward?' his wife asked.

The woman pulled out a crumpled copy of the previous week's *Springvale Leader* newspaper from a shopping bag. 'Here, see the headline on the first page: "*Reward offered for any information on missing cash.*" She shoved it back into the bag when she saw Detective Gomez approaching.

Feeling helpless, Phong pointed to the abandoned truck across the road with its cabin covered in graffiti. He had noticed in passing on his previous visit there.

'That's a likely spot,' he stammered as a crow

flew out from the interior of the open cabin.

'What? You can't be serious?'

Phong was emboldened by sudden logic. 'If the money was hidden on the property, the bad guys would have found it by now. No ways, they'd think of searching the truck.'

Detective Gomez frowned but then turned to her team.

'Right, let's get with it and empty the cabin.' She put on her gloves and facemask. 'You people there, get back. You are hindering police work.'

Two police climbed into the cabin and threw out household junk dumped by residents living nearby. But no sign of the money. Some of the spectators were taking photos of the drama in spite of being warned not to by the police.

'Detective Gomez, Detective Gomez!' called out the third policeman hidden from view.

Detective Gomez was stepping back into the street and making toward Phong, looking sweaty and frustrated. The urgency and excitement of the policeman stopped her in her tracks.

'What's up Constable Jones?' she said. The remaining two policemen stopped throwing the trash back into the cabin and rushed to their mate. A few bold spectators also ducked around the truck, not wanting to miss anything. So did Phong and his wife.

Detective Gomez was at Constable Jones's side

as he pulled out a large soiled hessian sack from under the bonnet. Another policeman exclaimed that the engine, in fact, had been removed to make room for the sack. From barely visible markings, it was deduced that the hessian had originated in China.

Constable,' said Detective Gomez 'careful you don't mess up any evidence.' As eager as the others to see what the sack contained, she pushed closer. It readily gave way to reveal several fully laden black plastic bags, each carefully tied with ladies' stockings. The first plastic bag broke as the knots were being opened. Bundles of Australian dollars fell out. A huge 'WOW' went up from the crowd, and simultaneously their iPhones began capturing the rare event.

Phong couldn't believe his eyes. Blinded by emotion and a great sense of relief, he smothered his wife in a fierce embrace. People near him seemed puzzled at his excitement and joy. Surely the money couldn't belong to him?

~

'Come on you two, get in, let's go to the police station and settle matters,' said Detective Gomez, smiling, as she got into her car. 'It shouldn't take long. The SOS note mentioned in your statement should be proof enough of your innocence – that's if you still have it and forensics can establish it is authentic. And if you're lucky, you may claim a four thousand dollar reward.'

Phong was overwhelmed. His thoughts were of his late mother and her murdered generous friend Rosalyn.

'You did well, dear,' whispered his wife.

~

MAKE THE MOMENT LAST

We'll arrive there
Soon enough,
Young like you
Or old like me.
So why hurry,
Why rush?
Just make the moment last.
(Slow down, you moving too fast
You got to make the morning last.
Feeling Groovy – Simon & Garfunkel)

RUPTURE

Our six-week camping trip in Eastern Canada was over. Brian, Monty and I, all in our late '70s, had found it a thoroughly enjoyable and uplifting experience. Our long friendship was energised. Such fun and laughter, such camaraderie.

After a short coffee break in Kington-on-St. Lawrence, we set off for Toronto in a buoyant mood. Towing a campervan some seven thousand kilometres had been a challenge. But in two hours we'd be home tucking into a lavish dinner, which Brian had requested of his wife. Although it was a Sunday afternoon, the highway was as busy as on any working day. Crowds of people were hastening back home. Monty, who was driving cautioned: 'We ain't home, mate, 'til we're home'. We laughed in unison.

Monty and Brian had first met in the 60s in Central Africa as high school teachers and soon became fast friends. On retirement, both settled in Canada with their wives and children. They'd gone on many camping trips together. So their bond of friendship was forged from challenge and adventure. On the other hand, I was an outsider and a novice to camping. I had migrated to Australia from Africa. It was at Brian's invitation, I'd flown to Canada to join him and Monty on an 'old timers' camping spree – to experience our very own lived version of *City Slickers*, the movie.

I was comfortably seated at the back of the 4-wheel drive listening to their unrelenting banter. Monty was, as usual, abrasive and loving it. Brian was left pleading his case, attempting to score points with emphatic gestures.

~

They were chalk and cheese: so different in interests and habits and even in their worldviews. In appearance, Monty was squat with a round face and frizzy greying hair. He wore spectacles, and was gifted with an infectious laughter, but confessed that strangers often thought he was angry because of his querulous-sounding voice. He loved his shorts, t-shirt and sandals, while his friend wore tight-fitting faded jeans frayed at the knee. Brian was tall and frail-looking with a pouting lower lip and unruly fringe of white wispy hair, which strayed from the back of his neck all the way to his Adam's apple. He was never without his Sherlock Holmes cap, and tended to speak in a soft, apologetic manner, his speech peppered with 'you see'.

Monty was driving at 120 km, ten kilometres above the speed limit on a six-lane highway, making Brian, a cautious driver, quite nervous. Brian cast furtive glances at the speedo-meter, but said nothing. I'll let them be, I thought. After all, they've been pals for almost half a century. For my part, I was enchanted by the Canadian landscape, the rugged hills covered in mountain ash, intensely dense and green and interspersed with sudden flashes of blue. Couldn't tell if these were inlets, bays, lakes or expansive rivers.

My drifting reverie burst like a bubble when I heard Brian say 'Believe me, Monty, it's nothing. The campervan always does this on the road, you see.'

'Listen to that sound Brian,' Monty retorted. 'Definitely not good. You're telling me it's *no problem*? Get real, man!'

I couldn't guess if Monty was annoyed or alarmed.

Brian lisped defensively. 'It's my vehicle and my campervan. I should know.'

'There! There! Hear that? Is that nothing?' Monty demanded.

I sat up and listened intently but heard nothing to alarm me. The next moment, Monty brought the vehicle to a gradual halt on a bridge where, fortunately, the shoulder was broad enough to minimise the risk of us being hit by traffic.

Brian jumped out to inspect both the 4-wheel drive and the campervan. He called out that the metal step of the campervan, which moved in and out on tracks much like a drawer, had come loose.

I wound down the window and leant out. 'Can you fix it?'

'Yeah,' he gave the jutting metal strip a firm kick to drive it back into its carriage. 'There, it's done. Shouldn't cause trouble again.' But just to be sure, he secured the step in position with a piece of wire, before jumping back into the car and giving Monty a smug smile.

'You absolutely sure the problem's fixed?' Monty was unconvinced.

'I think so,' Brian said, his certainty sorely tested.

The moment we moved again, a fractured metallic sound emanated from my side of the campervan. We all tensed.

'OK, you guys get out and have another look,' instructed an exasperated Monty.

Brian deflated.

Monty rolled the car backwards and forwards a couple of metres. I squatted alongside the campervan, listening for the harsh sound again in an attempt to identify its source. 'If it's not a loose bracket of some sort,' I speculated, 'it's got to be something like a wire caught on the underside.'

On closer inspection, Brian and I noticed that the problem was with the right-side wheel on the campervan. Three lugs were loose and spinning but still holding. I struck a cheerful note. 'Aren't we bloody lucky. We'd have been goners had the wheel spun off the hub.'

Brian looked sheepish, but said nothing.

It began to drizzle. Rain and I don't mix. I wasn't exactly excited standing in the open on a gusty, grey afternoon intimidated by endless screaming traffic just metres away. I pitched in to help, desperate to get moving again as soon as possible.

'Okay, okay,' said Brian, as if he were giving himself a pep talk in the hope of reclaiming control. 'This is what we'll do. I'll remove and replace the wheel with the spare. Help me get the jack and tool-kit from the boot.' I jumped to it.

Brian jacked up the campervan. He was obviously keen to inspire us with his skill and confidence. However, he failed to remove any of the nuts as they spun with the loosened lugs. The explanation was simple and alarming. Upon feeling behind the wheel itself, I discovered that the welding, which secured the lug heads to the hub, had fractured. Frustration and anxiety clouded

Brian's face. But he did not wish to be defeated, nor lose face.

Time was slipping by.

Monty looked disgruntled and stood removed from the action.

'You're wasting your time,' he ranted. 'Can't you see it's not fixable?' He repeated himself while rocking on his feet, hands thrust deep in his trouser pockets.

Brian continued fiddling undeterred, vice-grip in one hand and a spanner in the other. He mumbled under his breath. Perhaps he was urging himself not to give up.

Monty's attitude was getting on my nerves. 'It's not broken, Monty,' I said with as much patience as I could muster. 'The lugs have only worked themselves loose. Come and feel for yourself. The heads are spinning at the back.' I wondered if he was overly anxious about our precarious situation, and this was his way of coping – being negative and unhelpful. 'Why don't you go and find some help?' I suggested. 'You're good at that.'

'That's a very good idea,' agreed Brian as he stood up and gazed across the moving traffic, towards and over the opposite side of the bridge. 'Looks like there may be a business precinct there, even a garage.'

All I could see was a glum building with a brash sign "Fireworks Sold Here".

We unhitched the 4-wheel drive from the campervan and Monty drove off without a word.

~

There was little to be done now but wait. The drizzle had been only a brief tease, but the gloom of the overcast sky persisted, deepening as the day edged toward evening. It infected my mood. Brian continued to fiddle with his spanners after phoning his wife. She had berated him, he said, insisting that the breakdown was entirely our fault, a consequence of our hasty and careless preparations before setting off on our foolish adventure. 'In any case,' she had asked, 'what were you stupid old-timers trying to prove?'

Monty returned within half an hour, all smiles. He had found a garage, he said, and the garage attendant had helped him contact an off-duty motor mechanic who was also a tow truck owner. The mechanic would be with us shortly. Brian worried what he would charge for the service, it being a Sunday. And I wondered what we'd do if the campervan had to be towed to a workshop and kept there until next working day.

'Oh my god,' Brian moaned, 'don't even go there. My wife will likely kill me!'

'That'll be well-deserved, Brian,' chirped Monty, 'considering I stand to miss my flight home tonight because of you and your campervan.'

I considered this comment hurtful and uncalled

for.

The arrival of the mechanic was timely in averting an escalation in tension. The man parked his ute close behind the campervan. He was large, rough-looking and tattooed like a bikie. Almost bald. Surly. In shorts.

Monty's smile of achievement evaporated. Brian hastened to introduce himself and thank him for responding, and directed him to the problem.

The mechanic grunted, had a cursory look at the errant tyre, and returned to his ute. He opened the door of the cabin, which revealed shelves of tools and mechanical equipment of all shapes and sizes. We three looked on with interest. He didn't bother to attack the ceased nuts. Instead, he simply removed the damaged tyre within minutes by taking out the hub cylinder itself. The tyre was out as a single unit with the wheel rim, lugs and seized nuts intact.

Smart fellow. Certainly knows his job, I thought.

Clutching the tyre in one hand like a toy, he made for the ute. 'Workshop job,' he shouted over his shoulder. 'Take a while. Have the spare out for me when I return.'

'Thanks,' we called out, much relieved. 'Any chance you'll be done by eight?' asked a worried Monty. 'I have a plane to catch tonight.'

The mechanic closed the cabin and turned to confront us. Using a rag, he wiped the grease off his hands in a deliberate manner and grinned in a mean sort of way. I felt uneasy.

'Whoever changed the tyre the last time was clueless. Messed up the job. Damage likely cost you big time.'

Brian clasped his head in his palms and groaned. 'That can't be!'

'What, you don't believe me?' the mechanic sneered, opening the cabin again. He removed the damaged wheel and thrust it to the ground in a gesture of annoyance. He nudged the tyre with his foot to make his point. 'This side of the tyre with the air-pressure valve always faces out. Your tyre was installed back-to-front. Get it? That's what caused it.' At that the man flung the tyre back into the back of the ute and drove off.

The revelation stunned us. Brian, distraught and tongue-tied with humiliation retired to his 4-wheel drive and shut himself in the back seat. Monty fumed and fretted, stomping and swearing, '*You mumpara! You mumpara!*' I was caught between alarm and amusement. I had no idea what 'mumpara' meant but the expletive seemed to carry sufficient potency to help Monty discharge his anger into the night air. The next moment, he strode decidedly to the 4-wheel drive, removed his swag and backpack from the boot and walked past me into the night, rebuffing my pleas not to do so.

~

I felt strangely unsettled by my sudden predicament. Brian and Monty, my hosts, had together provided me comfort and safety in Canada. We had bonded like brothers. Now, only uncertainty prevailed. I became intensely aware of standing alone in encroaching darkness in a foreign land far from Melbourne.

I zipped my jacket to the chin to ward off the chill and mosquitoes, and went looking for Brian, all the while contemplating the tenuous nature of human relationships.

~

TRUMPET MAN

You're too much with yourself
Man;
Night and day
Dawn to dusk
Spouting your name.
Are you just a tweet
Or a new normal?
Madness with method.
We'll see.

ENCOUNTER IN OAKLEIGH CENTRAL

Most of life is constructed in the mind. Even the present moment is mainly made up of memory (Patti Miller).

'Who told you to be nurse in Casualty *and* a single-mum?' That's the sympathy I get from my son, Alex, whenever I moan about life. But tonight he promises to meet me and help with the shopping.

My right shoulder is playing up again. Arthritis. So here I am waiting opposite Coles in Oakleigh Central scanning the few shoppers, random stragglers, as they enter the plaza from two directions.

My attention is drawn to a woman leaning against one of the slatted wooden seats nearby. She is a solitary old woman going about her life on a Sunday evening in a deserted shopping plaza at an hour when most people are home enjoying the butt-end of the day. Perhaps even wishing Monday would never come.

She casts troubled glances at the huddle of grey plastic bags on one end of the bench then at her crammed cart by her side. Like her, the cart has seen better days, the frayed corners of the tartan bag visible even from this distance.

The woman ponders her bags yet again, appears tentative then picks up and separates them individually as if to confirm how many there actually are, all the while just standing at the unoccupied bench. She unzips the cart's cover-flap with unsteady fingers. Two large rings adorn her hand. She pulls out a couple of plastic bags from the top and then forces them back in, creating a little space. With effort, she manages to get two more bags in. But then the zip refuses to engage. She straightens up as much as this is possible for one with a pronounced stoop and takes her hands off the cart. Totally lost in the challenge of the moment, she seems oblivious of her surroundings – and of me standing only a few paces away! I'm the unsuspected witness to someone's very personal situation. Absorbed in this way, I quite forget the frustration of waiting for Alex.

I'm staring. I know I shouldn't. It's her amazing

shaggy hair that first sets me off: burnt ochre - very likely a wig. It reminds me of the colour of a dust haze sunrise over Uluru. This distinctive mop is making a bold statement on a very frail, little woman whose age is beyond conjecture. Simply ancient, I'd say. Shrunken and ravaged by time, her face is rather bird-like, pallid and heavily weathered. Her choice of fierce ruby lipstick is an assertion of her vital presence. 'See, I'm still alive. Not done yet,' the old woman appears to be saying.

I surmise that, like me, she's definitely waiting for someone. Why else would she be checking the time repeatedly? And why remain standing at an unoccupied bench if not mentally ready for a quick departure any second now?

Where can Alexis be? I worry, looking about.

Hardly any shoppers now. An Asian woman walks briskly towards Coles with her two little ones scampering behind her, barely keeping up. But then my attention returns to my primary fascination.

The woman pulls back the left sleeve of her brown jacket to check the time yet again. Her wristwatch appears rather large and heavy to sit on such a frail and slender wrist. The brown jacket is over a pink t-shirt, baggy blue jeans and Nike sneakers. I glance at my own beige slacks and brown jacket and wonder where the colour in my life has disappeared to. Clearly this woman's not defeated by age. Fashion conscious. Good for her! I imagine her taking pride at the mirror before leaving home.

~

'Hello, Mum. Sorry I'm late. Mike, my mate, held me up.' He's panting. Sloppily dressed as if he slept in the shorts and vest he has on. Wouldn't surprise me in the least. Shoe laces undone. It seems to be the fashion.

'Oh, I hadn't noticed, dear.'

Alexis glances at my face, quite puzzled. True, I'm a stickler for keeping time. As a sole parent, I keep him on a tight rein.

'Why do you have to go on and on all the time?' Alex would shout at times in annoyance. Like father like son, I'd remind myself.

'Here's the list, Son. You go ahead and start. I'll join you after visiting the *Ladies*. Remember to get a trolley.'

In reality, I wish to linger a little longer at my observation post to see who comes to pick up this woman who intrigues me.

I return from the *Ladies* as quickly as I can. The woman's still there. But then to my utter astonishment, she collects her shopping bags in one hand, clutches the trolley with the other, and gets moving – with just a last cursory glance at the vacant bench, careful not to leave any valuables behind. It's not as if she appears frustrated in any way that no one has come for her. Nor does she show any sign of doubt or worry about how she will make it home unaided, at this hour – especially with her weighty purchases. If anything, she sets off with resolve as if this is what she intended to do all along. Was she simply counting the minutes, resting in the moment before giving into the inevitable flow of her life?

I suppress an urge to rush out and block her way. 'You can't just leave like this! Explain yourself! Why aren't you waiting? What's really happening? I need to know!' But I don't move. I simply let her go.

Alex waves from the other side of the checkout nearest me. I wave back. He casts me one of his withering looks of impatience as he clutches the handle of an almost empty trolley. I hurry, squeezing past sullen-looking customers lined up at the checkout.

~

Much time has passed since that remarkable encounter. I continue to make regular sorties to Oakleigh Central. My attention always drifts to that slatted wooden bench. Isn't it odd that I've not seen it vacant since? The bench, I mean. Not even at night. On most occasions, it would be fully taken by forlorn shoppers seated shoulder-to-shoulder with little if any small talk. They seem burdened by aching limbs, by the pain of a meagre wallet, or even by life itself.

In that reflective mid-life mood, which often washes over me these days, I worry over the wrinkles appearing on the back of my hands and along my arms. They are like creeping fissures across a rain-starved landscape. My alarm bells alert me. I'm growing old, growing old! I wail in silence. No. I can't let this happen. I want a long life, long enough to see Alex marry a nice Greek girl. Long enough to enjoy the touch of grandchildren.

~

Like the memory of a field of dancing daffodils that swept away a poet's pervasive despair, in my moments of mid-life gloom, the lively image of an ochre-haired, red-lipped, designer-labelled ancient soul giving heaven her finger comes to me.

Ah, that's where the old woman stood! And this is where I stood and watched, helpless as she slipped into the night, taking her mysterious inner world of survival secrets with her. But then a shrill doubt insinuates itself. Was she just a figment of my imagination, crystallised now into an enduring memory? Did I really witness a living event or was it the mere movement of a distracted mind? One moment leaning into the next, mimicking the passage of my life onwards to its ultimate conclusion.

If only we could slow this relentless unfolding of our lives.

~

HUMAN CONDITION

Should I be fully present
When this body is turned into ash
And scattered to the wind,
Then will I have
Witnessed it all
At the heart of
Impermanence.

HAPPINESS AND JOY

Happiness is a rare thing,
A passing shower
On a parched land.
Joy is the face of sorrow
Caught in a shaft of sunlight
From a dark-laden sky.

NEERIM JUNCTION – A SPOT ON THE MAP

Christmas. As always, far too hectic and unnecessary.

To recover, Nisha, Viren, and I spent a few quiet nights in Neerim Junction, north of Warragul.

We arrived late in the afternoon after an arduous drive from Melbourne with sight-seeing stops at Walhalla, Thompson Dam and the Mount Baw Baw Alpine Village – an interesting back route through Icy Creek and Noojee. It was 35 degrees Celsius.

Our accommodation, acquired through Airbnb, proved to be pot luck. The timber house was at least seventy years old and had clearly seen better days. It had a red corrugated iron roof, waist-high picket fence painted white and a troublesome gate. Evidence of neglect and abandonment were everywhere – in the garden gone to feral weed and bush, and in the two iron sheds cluttered with broken furniture, bric-a-brac, a rusted trailer and caravan. Parts of the house were locked and shuttered. A peek through chinks in the drawn blinds revealed more domestic clutter. A house lives for people, I thought. Without their nurturing attention, it decays and dies from sheer neglect: much like pets.

Summer flies assailed us. As if to annoy us further, a few snuck into the house as we entered. Then we found that both the air-con and the ceiling fan were not functioning. Our elderly host from Melbourne, when phoned, responded with a touch of irritation. 'I don't know about the fan in the lounge. Don't think it was ever used. But the air con should work. Did you try it? You're sure?'

The stale smell of dogs and cats clung to the walls and blended with the damp odour of unaired carpets. We used a full can of air freshener to neutralise the air. I had to brush off fine animal hair from my track pants whenever I sat in the lounge.

Don't get me wrong: it was't all bad. The place was not a complete dump. The bed was comfortable, linen fresh and clean and the bathroom appeared to have been spruced up for Airbnb guests. And there was a functioning TV with good reception, so I didn't miss the ABC evening news and Nisha was able to watch Federer in the Hoffman Cup.

There were enough chairs in the place to seat a small party. This collection of fourteen mismatched chairs dispersed throughout the house, included a modern bucket seat and a sturdy wooden chair probably from a much earlier period, now worn, paint-splattered and banished to the pantry. Intrigued by this exhibition of chairs, I photographed each one, and later shared them with friends and family.

There were treasures to be discovered and mysteries to be speculated upon. When was the house built? Who had lived in it? How many owners had there been? How many generations called it home? And what had become of them? What clues could be gleaned from the paintings on the walls, the crockery and expired condiments in the cupboards and the jumble of books in the kitchen and pantry? I snooped and poked, peering into dark places.

The books excited me most. There were shelves of cookery books, including one entitled *Carrots Love Tomatoes and Roses Love Garlic.* But then I stumbled upon a collection of old and rare books in a cupboard in an unlit part of the passageway. I couldn't believe my eyes. *Captain Cook's Voyages of Discovery* (1906), *The Light of Asia – The Life and Teachings of Gautama* by Sir Edwin Arnold (1891), *Travels and Explorations in Southern Africa* by David

Livingstone (1905).

In addition to the books and chairs, there was an odd collection of framed picture-prints by known artists like Brett Whitely and also some amateur watercolour paintings. Most of these hung on Victorian-style picture rails. A few sat on mantle pieces and wall units.

~

I found myself most comfortable in the kitchen, which had an ample table in the centre and a large window over the sink with a generous view of ploughed land, grazing lots and the misty wooded hills beyond.

A large striking print, over a metre long and half a metre high, hung in the kitchen on a stretch of wall opposite the window. The label on the bottom right read *Zurich, Switzerland.* Whose initiative had it been to acquire this print and give it pride of place in the house? It was a strange picture of an unfurnished living room in tones of pale brown, pink and blue. Prominent in the picture were two girls – identical twins I'd say, about nine years of age with short-cropped hair. They were similarly dressed in beige vests and knickers, perhaps nightwear. In reality, the girls were ghost-like, since the painter had given them limbs but no solid torsos. One girl was kneeling on a bare slatted floor close to a fireplace central to the picture, engrossed in a bound hardcover book, oblivious of or indifferent to flames from the fireplace leaping out and licking at a pile of rare-looking leather-bound books.

The other twin stood more to the left facing away, her hands behind her back clutching a book visible to me. She was looking out across an open balcony, watching a hot-air balloon landing on a treacherous arctic landscape, its basket laden with flowering shrubs.

There was a long narrow passageway next to the fireplace leading to an open door and a vast ocean of rising water, which was about to flood the room and engulf the girls, the raging fire and whatever else there was inside. A ship could be seen on the ocean, ominous smoke bellowing from a single smoke stack. Blow me if I had any notion of what surrealistic message, if any, the artist was attempting to convey. I didn't even try.

~

The kitchen door opened onto a small timber decking crammed with an outdoor table and matching wrought-iron chairs that needed a good clean. A few slatted steps led me into the backyard. Initially, I went hunting for an outside tap and a hose to wash the car. No luck. The cottage was supplied by a rainwater tank, which was not substantial.

If I'd ever stumbled upon a totally abandoned backyard and garden, this was it. What was once carefully laid out and tended, had gone to bush and briar. Indulging my curiosity had its risks. I had to be mindful when working my way around not to step into holes concealed by grass, trip over a stump or graze past a thorny shrub.

I was struck by a resourceful bougainvillea bush using its many slender arms to reach upwards for sunlight. A lemon tree stood close by, burdened with unpicked fruit. Shattered clay pots were strewn near a fractured rusting wheelbarrow. I also came upon two open sheds facing each other at the very bottom of the garden, their access blocked by overgrowth. A rusted trailer filled the first shed and, barely visible in the other, was a caravan with flat tyres.

Yet again, I found myself musing. What was it like when real people with real names lived here, when their comings and goings would have given life to this place and kept the encroaching bush from laying claim? I attempted to imagine faces of those who owned and enjoyed the caravan, and the one who had planted the lemon tree. Had the backyard known the laughter of children? In reality, I will never know why the owners had given up on life here.

Everything here reminded me of a common human frailty – the mistaken hope that an accumulation of material things would keep us secure and earn us an identity: a sure buffer against the inevitable. Sadly, however, we all fall victim in time to illness, death, or some other calamity. Our material possessions then are abandoned, like an ancient Mayan city, only to be repossessed by the elements. Of course, in modern life the chances are that what we leave behind will be fought over and squandered by our offspring.

~

There was an all-purpose shop next door, which sold petrol from a unit installed on the pavement. Anyone wanting to fill up had to alert the attendant who came out, unlocked the pump and served the customer. The owner was a taciturn middle-aged Australian unwilling to engage in chitchat. Perhaps he was not comfortable to have dark-skinned people encroach his comfort zone.

Neerim Junction was, in reality, no more than a strip of houses, a shop and a community hall strung along a through-road with constant heavy traffic. It was not the safest place for brisk morning walks. Of course, there was a pavement which serviced no more than five houses in the one direction and four in the other. Hence, each of my power walks ended abruptly – like walking into a brick wall.

Late one morning, I crossed the road and headed for a dirt track running along a dairy farm, determined to do a sensible walk. But the flies were equally determined to frustrate me. I kept them at bay by walking at a pace and, simultaneously, swishing a piece of twig across my face from shoulder to shoulder.

The gravel ended at a farm cottage a short distance away. Nearby stood two imposing crane-like pieces of machinery. While my breathing settled, I looked around intrigued and puzzled. Not a soul about. A herd of cows, black and white patched, basked lazily in the field. Except for bales of cut and bound hay scattered about, the field was bare of vegetation. A tall middle-aged woman emerged suddenly from within the quietness of the house.

'Are you lost?'

'No,' I said. 'Just on a walk. But what are those things?' I pointed to the alien-looking machinery stark against a clear morning sky.

'Oh, those? One is for harvesting hay, while the other rolls, compacts and encases each roll in green plastic.' She seemed not the least bothered by the flies all about her.

I nodded and smiled. I now knew how the rolls of hay were made. We got chatting and I mentioned my rare experience of tasting farm-fresh milk fifty years ago in South Africa. The memory of my overnight stay on a small family farm in Winterton near the Drakensberg Mountains was still vivid.

'Well, come in and try the milk I've just collected from my dairy.'

This glass of fresh dairy milk tasted especially rich and full-bodied. A real treat.

~

Come Sunday 31 December, we tidied up our weekend home in readiness to depart later in the morning. No more rain and mist. Just a chilly morning with a clear sky with promise. But my tummy complained after a breakfast of leftovers from the fridge, affecting my mood. Nisha chatted about her week ahead: work plans and scheduled family commitments. Viren had the card game 'rummy' on his mind. He'd been the top scorer in our daily card marathon since we arrived.

'Could we fit in a game before we go?' He smiled with mischief.

It interested me that we'd become quite comfortable in this house. We no longer noticed the smells or the animal hair and we no longer grumbled about any shortcomings. Although it was quite cold at night, we had managed without heating, not persuaded to light the fire in the lounge. What was it? Had we taken on the smells, adjusted to the place, or simply become more accommodating?

What do you think?

IF I COME AGAIN

If I come again
Will you consider,
Will you promise
To plant acorns with me
On the way to London,
Sit under a tree and
Sing songs of praise
To lost worlds,
Fly to John O'Groats to see the
Sunset
And be back in Brighton
For dinner?
Whatever!
Should I come again
For God's sake

Let’s do something
Profound and meaningful,
Like sitting in the mid-day sun
At Hyde Park
Celebrating our last HURRAH!

SUN, SAND AND SEA CHANGE

Flo's first camp

Yay, we're here, my first ever sea-side camping trip.

I leapt from the Land Cruiser as soon as Daddy stopped and raced down to the water's edge. The rippled sand felt firm and cool. Wave after wave rushed towards me, only to break, frothing a little way away. I was a little scared and waited for Daddy.

'Daddy, watch me play.' At first, I waded into ankle-deep water. I jumped each time the chilly water rose up my legs. 'Yay!'

'Careful, Flo,'

After a while, Daddy called out 'Okay, that's enough for now.'

'But Daaad….'

'You'll have lots more opportunity, my girl, over the next few days. Come help me set up before dark.'

'But where's Lake Alexandrina?'

'It's on the other side of that ridge over there, love,' Daddy said pointing to a campervan on the hill. 'We'll pitch our tent near that campervan.'

The sun was sinking into the sea, lighting up the clouds nearby. A tall woman like Nanna was unpacking stuff from the campervan onto a wooden table.

'Hello there,' she called out. 'I'm Sue.'

'I'm Herb and this is my daughter, Flo.'

'Ebb and Flow? Really?' she chuckled and continued unpacking.

'It's my birthday today,' I said.

She looked up and smiled. 'How lovely. And…?'

'And I'm seven.'

'Come by later and I'll have some toasted marshmallows for you, young lady.'

Herb grieves for Flo.

Our camping days came to an abrupt end six years ago when Flo got diagnosed. 'But she's only thirteen,' I said to the doctor, 'our only child.'

Fear arrived uninvited and burrowed itself into the pit of my stomach, and my freaking life shifted for ever.

'Anorexia' the doctor said in a monotone. My

wife and I had taken Flo for a medical on the insistence of the school. A scream ballooned up in me. Flo sat expressionless. The doctor scowled at Amy like she had failed as a mother. Probably, as a nurse, she may have suspected it but not told me. It was beyond belief that a lively fun-loving, outdoor girl like Flo with an enormous zest for life would fall victim to such a nasty illness.

An ominous silence took hold as we walked back to our Land Cruiser.

'You should have seen it coming, Herb,' said Amy in a bitter tone even before I unlocked the car. 'You were at home with her most holidays and weekends while I worked. And what do you do but turn her into a tomboy? Just see how she dresses. I feel ashamed.'

'Only because you gave more time to your nursing job than to mothering.'

'Stop fighting over me. Please!' said Flo, wringing her hands.

Our disagreement persisted for over six years while Flo made herself invisible, wasting away unnoticed until it was almost too late.

Weariness and the first signs of a cold drove me to bed around midnight. Before then I gulped a hot toddy. It was Amy's turn to keep vigil, a routine we followed whenever Flo had a weekend release from the Adolescent Recovery Unit.

Soon I drifted into a restless slumber. I found

myself wading in surreal waters. Demons, ensnared in flotsam and jetsam, struggled to break free and get me. I flung my arms about like an inexperienced surfer who'd lost his balance.

'For God sake Herb, wake up. Heeeerb.'

I sat up in fright. Amy's face appeared through a haze. A faulty neon lit up the wall clock in eerie flashes. It was only 5 am.

'It's Flo.'

'What? What's happened?' I jumped out and fumbled for my glasses. Uneven snoring from the next room assured me Flo was definitely asleep. Amy read my puzzled look.

'Yes, yes she's asleep now. It's only because I stood over her until she finished her glass of milk. She's become so oppositional, even threatened harming herself if I persisted. She's out to give me a heart attack, I tell you. *Do* something or I'll crack.'

'No, our Flo's not about to self-harm, love. Believe me, she's a survivor.' I remembered Flo as a kid taken by a sudden backwash at Lake Alexandrina but making it to shore all on her own while I stood at the water's edge frozen.

'You're impossible, Herb,' she said wiping away angry tears.

I handed her a wad of tissues and drew her into a fierce embrace, something I hadn't done in years. 'There's got to be a way to keep her safe. What if I return her to the Adolescent Recovery Unit first thing in the morning?'

This suggestion infuriated Amy further. She pulled away. 'Years in and out of hospitals, emergency wards, recovery units and psychiatric care,' she rattled off. 'What good has all this done her? And you persist.'

'Well, you tell me what should I do?' I said as I fought to get into my pants.

'Keep your voice down,' Amy said moving across to the window. She stood motionless staring out, as if attempting to understand the ways of the universe. The Milky Way an eternal ocean, remote and awesome, was fast fading as dawn asserted itself.

~

'Dad! Mum! Where are you?' It was Flo's querulous voice, sounding as if it was coming across an ocean.

'Coming, love,' Amy called out. I rushed for the door, but she stopped me.

'What's it now?' I said brushing away her hold.

'Dreamt of camping at Lake Alexandrina.'

'Lake Alexandrina?'

'Top of her wish list, she says. You're the one who got her addicted to the sea and surf in all weather. Have you forgotten?'

'Give me a break, honey. And don't keep harping that we're about to lose Flo. In any case, we've not camped in South Australia since Flo was little.

'You sort that out with Daddy's girl then. I'm merely relaying her wish.'

Flo wins over Herb

The moment Dad got to my bed I clutched his hand and drew him close.

'Can we go to Lake Alexandrina?' I pleaded.

'No. Not if you don't eat healthy and get stronger. You're even too weak to get yourself to the loo without help. I can't bear to see you like this, love.

'But Dad,' I said hoarsely, please don't go on about me eating. It pisses me off. You know very well I simply can't keep anything down. It's not my fault. I dreamt the other night we were there again, Dad, you and I. The water was lapping and the wet sand was under my feet. So cold. You remember?'

He hugged me. His glasses misted over. Dad was worried I wasn't well enough to cope with a two-day drive to the coast, but he'd check with Dr Bruce he promised. I was disappointed at Dad's reluctance, but said nothing.

'You needn't look all glum' said Mum.

'But you don't understand why I need to go.'

Later Dad took me to The Recovery Unit. Dr Bruce was a woman with authority written across her face. I was hoping Dad would do the talking.

'At nineteen, you should speak for yourself. Anyway, Mum believes I've spoilt you rotten.

Maybe she's right.'

'I'm not too excited about this trip, Flo,' said Dr Bruce, leaning back in her chair. My tummy hurt and made weird sounds. 'But I see how eager you are. All those happy memories camping at Lake Alexandrina. Good memories are good medicine,' she said.

I waited.

Dr Bruce then spoke directly to me. 'The journey can be quite risky unless you rest, eat and take in lots of liquid. Don't exert your-self. You are responsible for your health, but remember you will hurt those who most love you if you don't take charge of your recovery.'

My weekend pass was extended for a further five days. Dad was handed a referral note to the Adelaide Women's Hospital to use in an emergency.

Herb Drives Flo to Lake Alexandrina

By the afternoon, I had the Land Cruiser packed and ready. Amy remained sullen but took charge of the packing, making sure we had everything. On occasions like this, her fastidious nurse's training came in handy. I wished she'd go with us.

'You know I can't cope with long distance travel,' Amy said.

'But we'll make frequent stops.'

'Our last drive to the Gold Coast was just awful. I was sick as a dog. In any case, I can't stomach camping. So that's the end of it.'

I was up by 4am the next morning, still feeling anxious about doing the trip without Amy. We had prepared comfortable bedding for Flo in the back of the Land Cruiser. With little effort I carried her, still drowsy, and lowered her onto the bedding. Frighteningly light, she snuggled into her blanket, sighed and promptly fell asleep.

My head ached and my chest felt tight as I set off. It was five days to Christmas. I'd have rather preferred to be home with a grumpy wife. But still.

Alice Springs was eerily still under a morning haze. Another scorcher was predicted. The Stuart Highway to Adelaide was a withering, monotonous stretch.

~

I pictured a freckled-face Flo sitting beside me in shorts and t-shirt adjusting her cap as she peered into the rear-view mirror, leaning into me in the process. She'd constantly fidgeted with one thing or the other – flipping through the CDs, changing discs or pouring over the route map. She'd had endless questions, too. She was eager to know everything about camping and Lake Alexandrina. She checked I was alert and awake by handing me the water bottle at intervals. We were supremely happy then, humming, laughing and ragging each other. I had little care in the world. Flo had just turned seven. That's when she first saw the ocean.

A road-train hooted and I gave way. I'd been driving for three hours. I pulled up briefly at a petrol station at Marla to phone Amy. Flo appeared feverish. I thought it was odd and held a palm against her nose to confirm her breathing. Her face and hair were sweaty. I cooled her down with wet wipes and offered her water. She groaned and pushed the bottle away, causing some water to spill onto her. Is this the moment I should consider turning back? But I dismissed the thought and continued towards Coober Pedy, our overnight stop. I estimated we'd be there late afternoon.

I felt weary. My body ached. A good sleep and a clear head were what I needed.

Flo had hardly stirred. I pulled over on a shoulder along a clear stretch of the highway to see how she was fairing. 'Flo, babe,' I whispered in her ear. I shook her by the shoulder. 'Can you hear me? It's Dad. Wake up.' She didn't respond. What now? Was Amy right all along? Was Flo sicker than I was prepared to admit? I'd better get Flo to the Adelaide satellite hospital in Port Augusta, I decided. A rest stop in Coober Pedy was now out of the question, and Lake Alexandrina was no longer in my sights.

The fatigue I'd felt only a little earlier evaporated. I sat leaning into the steering wheel driven by a single purpose.

Near nine in the evening I hit the outskirts of Adelaide, having driven non-stop. Drenched in perspiration, I pulled up at the very first service station I spotted for directions to the hospital.

Flo awakes rested

Why'd we stop?

Worried, I knelt on my bedding and peered out the rear window. I spotted Dad hurrying back from somewhere. I tapped on the window. He froze and peered back, his mouth open as if he'd seen a ghost.

'Is there a problem, Dad? Let's keep moving.'

'Are you okay? Are you well?' he said feeling my face and tousling my hair.

'Why? I just had the most amazing sleep, that's all.'

'Gosh, you certainly gave me a fright. I was about to rush you to the hospital here. To be on the safe side, I think we should still check you out.'

'No Dad,' I protested. 'We're wasting time. But the loo first, if you don't mind.'

As I was helped out, my head spun and knees gave way. The lady attendant at the service station came running over. 'Oh my God, what's happened? Shall I call the ambulance?'

'No, no. I don't need that. Not now,' I whispered, 'but can you help me to the Ladies?' She seemed relieved to hear me speak. But Dad appeared strangely uptight, muttering under his breath as he and the lady carted me to the toilet.

'Thanks,' Dad called out as the lady attendant

returned to her post.

~

As soon as we got moving, I felt like throwing up. Dad hastily pulled into a private dirt road. I sat up and, after a burp or two, felt much better.

'Let's go. Lake Alexandrina, here we come,' I sang, my voice rasping and breaking into a cough. But Dad just stood before me, feet apart. His stubbled face drawn and flushed, his hands thrust into his pockets. I sensed something ominous. My tummy rumbled.

'Look here, my girl,' he began, 'like Mum, I've just about had enough.' His pointing finger said it all. 'I'm worn to the bone. I'll take no more nonsense from you. Hear me?' His laboured breathing frightened me more than did his words.

'Why're you being mean to me?'

'No more whining and no more Lake Alexandrina.' He got back into the land cruiser.

I froze. I felt a distance come between Dad and me like I'd not known before. I found myself rocking as I knelt on my bedding.

Herb decides

'Okay, this is what we'll do,' I said making it clear I wasn't in the mood for negotiation. We'll take a short detour to the beach on the way to the hospital. Right? We'll bed the night in a local motel and make an early start for Alice Springs tomorrow.

Camping is definitely out.'

'Ooooh.'

'Lake Alexandrina will always be there.' I said a little short of sympathy.

The muffled sound of surf was unmistakable from the dirt road, but the ocean itself was hidden by saltbushes and dunes. I wound down all the windows. 'Can you hear the surf?' I said, thinking Flo would be roused and excited. But not so.

A partial moon was rising over the ocean. The loose sand was difficult to walk on, so I carried Flo to the water's edge. Flo, no heavier than a sack of polystyrene beads, remained quiet and compliant. The tide was on its way in. I waded into a large rock pool and lowered myself onto a rock, sitting with my legs outstretched and Flo propped up between them, her head resting on my chest. We sat this way for several minutes without a word being spoken until I broke into a spate of yawning.

'Are you done, Flo? Can we move now?'

'Nooo. Let's stay just a little longer? I want to float on my back. Help me, please.'

I let her try, but kept a wary eye wondering what was to become of her. As darkness crept in, the almost spent moon was joined by a sprinkle of stars. I had the dreaded thought that Amy, Flo and I had drifted apart. And there was little I could do. I realised, too, that Flo was no longer my *little girl* but a young woman. If only she'd let me get to know her all over again. If only.

Flo reflects

It's unreal. I'm floating and floating, and loving it. Loving the sound of waves, the darkness hugging me, and the specks of light in the distant sky. Yes, it's the same feeling I had at Lake Alexandrina. But then I completely lost it when I began hurting. If only I knew how to get well again. The only thing I'm certain of for now is I'm hungry. Bloody hungry. It's the salt air, I guess - the very best medicine.

Herb is at peace

A sea bird circled high above, hanging in mid-air beyond the heaving waters, wings out-stretched and still, etched against a shimmering sky. We'd be driving back in oppressive heat. So what? Even the fear that had possessed me for so long had lifted. Flo appeared serene and rested. We chatted and enjoyed the drive back.

Christmas awaited us in Alice Springs.

~

TOMORROW

As light and warmth recede
Into the deepening shadows of dusk,
Joy gives way to regret,
Sadness
For pleasures and pain that's done.
Night beckons
With a resolute finger
Turning me in stillness,
In acceptance
In hope of finality
Not to rise again
No sun reborn
No morning dew
No existential woes.
Just this
Once rare and precious life.

SELF-INFLICTED PAIN OF THE WRITER'S KIND

It's debatable what's harder: to produce a piece of creative writing or to find someone willing to read a draft and give authentic feedback. I was pleased and relieved when Jude readily agreed to read my draft crime novella. After all, I argued, not only was he a good friend, but also a well-read and incisive member of a book club. I could certainly count on him to be objective in his feedback, yet encouraging. If he wished, he could do so over lunch. I'd shout him and we'd make it a social occasion. It should be fun, I thought. Little did I realise the day would end as it did.

'Who's that?' he said answering his phone on the first ring. Landline.

After his initial surprised, 'Oh, hello,' we

exchanged some pleasantries.

'Yep, I got your draft the other day. Read it over lunch. Has great potential.'

'Let's meet at Muffin Break then,' I said casually without letting on how keen I was to get his comments. 'Tomorrow at noon in Oakleigh Central opposite Woolworths?' I assured him that it was no more than a few minutes from the Station.

It was a short walk from home to Oakleigh Central. On the way, I speculated on how impressed Jude would be with my first piece of crime writing – with the very original title *For Goodness Sake, Don't Tell.* I pictured the conversation and me beaming with modest pride. After all, didn't I think this was my best effort at creative writing so far? On the other hand, if he was not immediately forthcoming, I'd egg him on a bit. But that would be sneaky, wouldn't it? Oh well, it couldn't be helped.

As I walked over the railway bridge on Golf Links Avenue, a train from the city halted at the Oakleigh Station for a moment and then continued on to Dandenong, passing under me.

Jude was standing against a pillar at Muffin Break and looking the other way as I came up behind him. It wasn't hard to make him out: tall and gangly, shoulder length straw-coloured hair held in place by a brimmed sunhat. I gave the tail end of his hair a slight tug. Startled, he turned around and appeared relieved it was only me.

'There you are,' he said grinning. His eyebrows, expansive beard and moustache were of the same hue as his hair, reminding me of a stubbled wheat field recently hand harvested.

'Waiting long?'

'Oh no, not too long,' he said peering down at me. 'Haven't been to Oakleigh in years, you know. So I went on a little look see,' he gestured with his hand, fingers thin and expressive. He transferred his bulky backpack from one shoulder to the other.

'Ready for lunch?'

'Yup.' An eager smile lit up his face. 'Lead the way.'

'There's pizza. Or would you rather explore what Eaton Mall has to offer?

'Oh, I'd rather settle for pizza anytime.'

I shivered as we stepped out onto the street and regretted not having carried a jacket. It didn't seem to bother Jude. All he had on was a well-worn white t-shirt and khaki workman's longs.

'What! Feeling cold? You can't be serious. I've a cardigan in my backpack if you don't mind getting it out. It's sure to fit you.' He turned his back to me. I unzipped his backpack and tugged at a large cardigan stuffed in like soiled washing. In the process, I dislodged pages of creased paper stapled together.

'Give me that,' said Jude hastily snatching it from me, but not before I glimpsed the scrawls all over and lines of writing bracketed or deleted. It was the draft copy of my precious crime novella, heavily edited. The thought of wine and pizza in good company was no longer that appealing.

'Haven't seen you at the book club in a while,' said Jude as if to distract me, his voice almost lost in the cacophony of people and traffic.

'Yeah. I've been indisposed lately. Writer's fever.'

'You don't say,' Jude chuckled.

In a few minutes we were at our chosen restaurant.

'Looks a nice enough place. Good choice, mate.'

'Let's take the table in the far corner,' I said, leading the way.

Jude slid his backpack to the floor. I felt relieved we'd decided on this place with such ease, considering the array of tempting cafés and restaurants in Eaton Mall.

While waiting to order, Jude reached down and pulled out the draft from his backpack and flipped over the pages as if he were deliberately filtering his comments.

The waiter, a portly middle-aged man with an Italian accent, set down Jude's glass of red and my gin and tonic. He assured us that the pizza was on its way.

'So, Jude, what do you think - all good or all bad?' I said after thanking him for his friendship and ready support. He chuckled and was dismissive, gesturing with his long-fingered hand and stroking his moustache.

'You know, I'm not really good at giving feedback – especially helpful ones.'

'Come on, your contributions in the book club were always pertinent and perceptive. So let's not be that modest now.'

'Yeah, but I'm more into historical stuff – military strategies and biographies, you know.'

Our pizza arrived. Its look and aroma were deadly as some would say. Jude immediately assaulted it single-mindedly, using his fork to draw a couple of pieces onto his plate with strands of melted cheese and topping trailing behind.

'Let's keep talking,' I said.

He nodded, licking the sauce off his lips and moustache.

'There's this nice descriptive bit at the beginning of your story,' said Jude. He rested his fork and knife for a moment and held up the creased draft in front of him. 'Here on the very first page. It's an image of a jug of fresh milk sitting on the kitchen table, straight from morning milking.'

I knew exactly what Jude was alluding to. In fact, I considered it an example of fine writing, which pleased me. I describe how beads of moisture trickled down a stainless-steel jug brimful of fresh milk.

'Well', continued Jude in an apologetic tone, 'fresh milk that's directly from a cow is naturally warm. Never chilled.'

'Really? Naturally warm?' I was floored. Two innocuous words, but they sounded like two strokes of Big Ben. Jude's hirsute face creased in smile.

'Gosh, Jude, I would never have known that, not even remotely.'

Jude took this as a cue to tell me of his early days growing up in country New South Wales. For my part, I was only half attentive as I was reflecting, instead, on the advice often given by accomplished writers to amateurs: do your research! Factual errors in a book, fiction or non-fiction, put off readers in a big way. It suggested ignorance or laxity on the part of the writer.

The waiter came over. 'Coffee?' he asked as he began clearing the table.

'Haven't decided yet,' Jude said feeling his moustache before giving it a cursory wipe with a serviette.

'I suggest we move somewhere quieter for coffee,' I said. 'It's such an effort for me to hear you.'

'Okay by me.'

'Ah, the sun's out,' observed Jude, his attention momentarily drawn to the sight of children romping outside. Eaton Mall was abuzz with lunchtime patrons, some engrossed in good cuisine and good company. Others looked lonely, distracted or decidedly bored. We found a cosy cafe on Chester Street. While waiting for the coffee to arrive, Jude returned to my manuscript.

'There's not much more I can say. On the whole, an interesting read,' he said, paging through the draft once more. 'The local setting does give it an authentic feel. A few typos and lapses in grammar here and there. Not too serious.'

'Thanks, but what about all the scrawled notes, page on page? Suggests a very thorough scrutiny, wouldn't you agree?'

'Yeah, but…. that only tells you how much I was drawn to it. I admire your guts. Nope. I don't have the courage to try my hand at writing.' He stirred his half-empty coffee cup as if it held his thoughts. 'I'd say there's much too much detail in some parts. It can lose the reader, you know.'

'Oh?'

'Yeah, like the shopping bit and smelly toilets.'

I stood up and took off Jude's cardigan and called for a glass of water.

'What else?'

'Well, the dialogue could be less formal. I guess you watch TV crime like Fargo or Janet King.'

'You mean my characters are wooden?' I said feebly. I pushed aside my coffee, now decidedly lukewarm, and glanced at my wristwatch.

'Yeah, it's about time I took off.'

'No, no I don't mean for you to stop, Jude. What useful comments. You're good.'

A bemused smile graced his entire face and lit up his pale grey eyes. 'Oh well, if you insist then … there's just one more thing you may wish to consider,' he said as an afterthought.

What now, I wondered with a little alarm. 'And what's that?' I rearranged the sachets in the sugar bowl.

'Mavis the detective, central to your story, puzzled me. Couldn't make sense of her chronic emotional insecurity and her anger over the bloke who took off after killing his mum and dad. Perhaps the reader would appreciate a bit of backstory here. But it's up to you. You're the writer.'

Was Jude being deliberately tentative or simply provocative, I puzzled. 'Now that's interesting. I'll certainly revisit it.' Bugger me if I'm expected to know the life history of each and every one of my fictional characters. Who am I – god?

I looked on as he tilted his cup and slurped the remaining froth and ran the back of his palm across his lips. Plaintive Greek music drifted in the air, faint and soporific. I was beginning to tire of the afternoon.

'Gosh,' said Jude as he checked the time on his iPhone. He handed me the draft with his comments before pulling out his wallet from his backpack. 'My turn to shout.' He kept talking until we reached

Oakleigh Station where he briskly hopped onto a waiting train as the doors were closing. His parting wave and smile blurred and disappeared in seconds.

~

As I walked home, Jude's counsel rang in my ears like an errant hornet. 'Keep to what you know. Crime writing is best left to crime writers. Don't add to the glut of crap around. If you ask me, crime is an overrated and overdone genre.'

I had chosen to ask a friend for feedback and received a withering but friendly admonition. Will I now ever call myself a writer, I wondered.

~

ACKNOWLEDGEMENTS

The stories and poems in this collection took shape over three years, having been worked and re-worked with the support of the Caulfield Writers Group and the Monash Writers Group. An additional valuable resource was Nicole Hayes and the participants of her Phoenix Park Creative Writing Class.

Kieran Carroll and Neerosh Mudaly often had the unenviable task of wading through my often poorly crafted first drafts and providing encouragement. You were both very generous with your precious time. Much appreciated.

I cannot thank Robert New and Sylvia Karakaltsas nearly enough for enlightening me on the steps I had to follow to eventually hold a printed copy of my book – the final product of a daunting and costly endeavour. They tolerated my ignorance of self-publishing with grace.

Leanne September assisted with preliminary work on a suitable cover design. Thank you.

Finally, I am greatly indebted to Josephine Burnell my copy editor who was painstakingly thorough.

ABOUT THE AUTHOR

Bala Mudaly was born in South Africa in 1938. He migrated with his wife to Australia thirty years ago, and continues to practice as a psychologist in Melbourne. He has particular interest in how characters in fiction come to life, take on a persona of their own and may even outlive their creator.

Bala's early interest in writing did not go much beyond the high school magazine. However, since 2015 Bala has dedicated himself to learning and mastering the art of creative writing.

Bala may be contacted at bala.mudaly@gmail.com

AFTERTHOUGHT

A piece of creative writing remains a work-in-progress. Never quite done. Yet there comes a time when the writer has to let it go and move on.

So, too, it is with one's life.

www.ingramcontent.com/pod-product-compliance
Lightning Source LLC
Chambersburg PA
CBHW030651110726
47901CB00002B/665

* 9 7 8 0 6 4 8 3 2 7 3 0 1 *